John Russell Coryell, Nick Carter

The American Marquis

Detective for Vengeance

John Russell Coryell, Nick Carter

The American Marquis
Detective for Vengeance

ISBN/EAN: 9783337397005

Printed in Europe, USA, Canada, Australia, Japan

Cover: Foto ©Andreas Hilbeck / pixelio.de

More available books at **www.hansebooks.com**

THE AMERICAN MARQUIS;

OR,

DETECTIVE FOR VENGEANCE,

A Story of a Masked Bride and a Husband's Ouest,

By Nick Carter,

Author of

"THE OLD DETECTIVE'S PUPIL," "THE WALL STREET HAUL,"
"THE CRIME OF A COUNTESS," ETC.

NEW YORK:
STREET & SMITH, Publishers,
29 Rose Street.

THE AMERICAN MARQUIS.

CHAPTER I.

A MASKED STRANGER.

A quaint old town is Morlaix, in Upper Britanny, and full of rambling streets and ancient houses.

Away at the end of the Rue Perelle, and standing in desolate solitude, as if waiting for the sleepy old town to catch up with it, is a dilapidated house.

It is abandoned now, and it ought to have been so half a century ago. But it was not.

Less than twenty years ago, had the townspeople been asked who lived there, they would have shrugged their shoulders and spread out their hands in good French fashion and said:

"An artist—an American. *Pauvre diable!*"

"That was all they knew. He was an artist, and an American; so, of course, he was a poor devil.

Clinton Hastings would have said something very like it, too, had his opinion of himself been asked.

More especially had he been asked, one wild November night, as he sat with his eyes intently fixed on the easel before him.

A young man, and a handsome one, too, in spite of the uncared for curling, brown beard which hid the whole lower part of his face. In spite of the threadbare clothes so carelessly worn; in spite of the half-reckless, half-gloomy, almost sneering expression hovering about the nostrils of his clear-cut nose and the corners of his clear gray eyes.

"Bah!" he muttered, scornfully thrusting his hands deeper into the pockets of his blouse and stretching his legs out like a pair of compasses, "I do nothing but dream! I love a shadow! Another man's wife, it may be! Ye gods and little fishes! I see a woman once; I paint her picture from memory; I sit and dream. Ay, and starve, too. Clinton Hastings, you are an ass!"

The cloth covering was angrily thrown over the ravishing face, and the artist went on muttering:

"Better look at your rejected picture, Clinton, my boy."

He disdainfully threw the cloth from a large piece of canvas, disclosing a landscape view.

Silently he looked at it for several minutes, holding a lamp so as to throw the light upon it.

Suddenly he started, and turned his head to listen.

He heard a soft footfall on the creaking stairs.

A grim smile lighted the gray eyes as Clinton held a dialogue with himself.

"A thief?

"Nothing to steal—except my picture——

"A beggar?

"Nothing to eat—except my picture.

"A friend?"

"*Mon Dieu!* I have none—except my picture."

The first two times he made his answer he nodded jeeringly at his landscape, but the last time he turned toward his portrait with a half-savage, half-ecstatic expression.

He was madly in love with a shadow!

A knock sounded on his door.

"Come in!"

The door opened wide, and a masked man, robed to his feet in a heavy cloak, stood framed in the door-way.

Whatever the young artist may have felt, he betrayed no emotion, but speaking with the utmost coolness and with ironical politeness, said:

"Ah! *Bon soir*, monsieur. What shall it be—my money or my life?"

"If I wanted money I would not come here. If I wanted your life I would wait a few days."

"Aha, Monsieur le Diable, I see you know me well. Who are you, then?"

"That is of no consequence."

"Is it not?' Well, *mon ami*, let me say to you two things. First, I do not like masked strangers to come to me at night. Second, if they do come I throw them down stairs."

The prospect of an encounter seemed to give the artist positive pleasure, and his eyes sparkled as he made a quick step forward.

"Stop!" said the stranger, coolly; "I know you can throw me down stairs to-night. You are stronger than I am. But what good would it do you? I could come here again a week hence."

"Ah, yes, I see," cried Clinton, with a short laugh. "You mean that in a week from now I shall be so feeble from starvation that I cannot throw you down."

"Exactly."

"I admire your forethought, but not your wisdom. You only make me more anxious to take advantage of the golden opportunity. It will give me great pleasure to throw you down stairs."

The artist was still smiling, but the reckless humor in him was shown in the quick way in which he laid hold of the stranger.

"You don't know yet what I came for, monsieur."

On the point of being thrown down stairs, the man in the mask was nevertheless quite cool.

"True," ejaculated Clinton, releasing the man; "I can learn that first and remove you afterward. Business before pleasure, you know. Sit down."

"Thank you."

"Shall I take off your mask, or will you save me the trouble?"

"Neither, if you please. You must, in fact, promise that you will not seek to penetrate my disguise, or I will not reveal my business."

"That promise will not prevent me from dropping you over the balusters, will it?"

"Oh, no. You may do that afterward, if you wish."

"All right, monsieur. You have my promise, and I wait eagerly for the happy moment when our interview shall have ended."

With mock politeness the artist sat down. The stranger began as if telling a story:

"Your name is Clinton Hastings; your picture was re-jected by the Academy; you are hungry now; unless you have aid you will starve to death; you have no friends—no hope."

Clinton bowed, smiled cheerfully, and said:

"As I have already partially suggested, you are, perhaps, the devil. I think I must use the window instead of the stairs. But go on; you interest me."

"To-morrow you may have ten thousand francs, if you will."

"Then you are really the devil, and it is my soul you want. Dear me! Now, I didn't suppose my soul was worth so much."

"Keep your soul; I only want your body for to-night."

"Ah, yes! I comprehend now; you wish me to kill some-body for you. Really, I am sorry the window is not higher."

"I am glad you can be so merry."

"So am I."

"My proposition is this: You are to marry a woman whose face you shall not see——"·

"Your family was born masked, then?"

"Whose name you shall not know, and whom you must leave as soon as the marriage ceremony is over."

"What a charming mystery! Why, it is like the good old times. But go on; you begin to amuse me."

"You will let me blindfold you, and take you to the place where the bride is. After the wedding I will give into your hands the ten thousand francs, and bring you back here, still blindfolded."

"Are you ready now? Shall I open the window?"

"Do you refuse? Starvation if you do, and plenty if you do not."

"Positively, monsieur, you mortify me. I knew, my-self, that I was a fool, but how on earth did you dis-cover it?"

"I do not understand you, monsieur."

"Shall I explain, and then drop him out, or shall I drop him out at once?"

The young artist asked himself this question so calmly that the masked man was visibly affected by it, and moved uneasily in his chair. Evidently his proposition had not been accepted, as he had expected. He affected com-posure, however.

"It would suit me better if you would explain first," he said.

"Well, I will, then. I know that no marriage that can be performed to-night will be legal, because banns must be published on two Sundays. Besides, no mayor would marry masked people. Besides, the woman's name would have to be mentioned. Will you walk to the window, or shall I carry you?"

"If those are your only objections, listen. The banns have been published as required by law."

"How could that be done?"

"I was so sure you would accept, that I had your name used."

"I wish you could realize my great grief that the window is so low."

"The mayor has consented to be in attendance and perform the ceremony, and I have four witnesses all ready. The woman's name I was going to ask you to shut your ears against, and the mayor has agreed to speak it softly."

"Your forethought makes me tremble."

"Why?"

"Because I fear you may have laid a feather bed under my window to fall on."

"Oh, come, now, monsieur, have done with jesting. I will reveal the mystery, suppressing only the names."

"Do not suppress the names on my account," interrupted the artist, who took a malicious pleasure in trifling with his strange visitor.

CHAPTER II.

A MYSTERIOUS RIDE.

"Our family comprises four brothers and a sister."

"Four of a kind, queen high!" said Clinton, interrupting.

"We are a noble family, but poor. A wealthy uncle, in dying, left his whole fortune to us equally; to be divided, however, only when our sister should marry.

"Our sister, unfortunately, is determined upon going into a convent.

"She has consented, however, to this marriage, with the understanding that, as soon as it is over, she may go to Austria, there to enter a convent.

"This is really all there is of it, monsieur. Surely you have all to gain, and nothing to lose."

"Is your sister good-looking?"

"What difference can it make to you if she is or not?"

"Answer my question."

"She is beautiful; but you may not see her face. Do you consent?"

"If you are poor, how can you give me ten thousand francs?"

"Ah, monsieur, ten thousand francs! What a sum is that? When I say poor, I mean poor for a noble family."

"Very well, then," said Clinton, who had come to a sudden resolve to see the adventure out, come what might of it. "But how am I to have the use of your services, and, the same time, drop you out of the window?"

"Oh," said the stranger, gayly, "we can postpone that."

"Two things," said Clinton. "I must have something to eat, and I must have some good clothes."

"Everything is prepared. In the carriage, which will be at the door in a minute, are all you ask for."

"How thoughtful of you!"

"This affair has been carefully planned."

"But suppose I had insisted on throwing you out of the window?"

"You would not have done it."

"Oh, but I was very near it."

"Well, then, this!"

The stranger threw aside his cloak, and showed a pistol in his hand.

Already suspecting that there was more in the adventure than appeared on the surface, Clinton now decided that he had entered on a hazardous enterprise.

If the stranger, who knew all, was prepared with weapons there must be danger.

Little difference did it make to Clinton, however. The more danger, the more excitement. Anyhow, he reasoned, he could be no worse off than he was.

The danger probably was his. He would be on the alert to ward it off.

While he was soliloquizing, the stranger had taken the lamp, held it in front of the window a few seconds, dropped it suddenly below the window, and repeated the signal twice.

A few moments later the noise of a carriage was heard outside.

"I will return, with the food and clothes," said the stranger, departing.

In a short time he was back, and Clinton was discussing a hearty meal, with as much calmness as if nothing unusual was on hand.

The clothes fitted to a nicety.

"You made a good guess, monsieur," said Clinton, as he noted the fit.

"It was not a guess; I had your measure."

"Oh!"

"Are you ready now?"

"Yes. Go down; I will follow in a few moments."

The stranger went down.

Clinton pulled aside the cloth from the portrait, gazed at it earnestly a while, and then, dropping on his knee before it, kissed it passionately.

"Beautiful creature!" he exclaimed; "insensible image! my happiness! my destruction! to you do I owe it that I have this night sold myself. Had I not wasted weeks mooning over your shadow, I would not now owe my life to a stranger's need. Fool as I am to have let you bring me to this, so, fool will I be to hold you accountable for the issue of this night's adventure."

So intense was the passion of this singular utterance, that it was hard to recognize in the speaker the reckless, sardonic artist of a moment before.

In another second the mood was changed, and with a mocking laugh, Clinton had tossed back the cloth over the sweet face, blown out the light, and dashed headlong down the pitchy dark staircase.

"What!" he exclaimed, as he sprang lightly out into the street; "only two horses for a mystery like this! Why, we ought to have four at least, and six would be none too many."

"Come, monsieur, we have no time to love. Will you enter?"

"Certainly, oh, man of mystery. But tell me first, is the driver masked?"

"He is. Why?"

"Why? Because in an adventure like this, the least you

could do would be to have a masked coachman.   I am sorry you neglected to have four horses, though."

"You are a strange man."

"You're another."

The man laughed softly.

They were rattling along at a good round pace by this time.

In a short while a soft country road was struck; and, as if waiting only for that, the driver spoke to his horses, and, like a flash, they sprang into a furious pace.

The carriage swayed and bounced, and the two men inside with difficulty kept their seats.

"If a thunder-storm would only come on now," said Clinton, "and we should fall over a cliff just as a flash of lightning broke through the black sky, how picturesque it would be!"

"Perhaps; but I should enjoy it best if I were out of the carriage.   You might be accommodated going back—at any rate as to the storm, for one is coming up."

"Maybe you will see to it that I am accommodated on the way back."

"Why should I?"

"I don't know."

Nothing more was said until, in about an hour, a stop was made, and new horses were put in.

"Where are we?" asked Clinton.

"Can't you tell?"

"No."

"I dont wan't you to.   I'll blindfold you now if you please."

Three times the horses were changed, and Clinton calculated that nearly fifty miles had been covered, and that it must be after midnight.

CHAPTER III.

A VISION OF LOVELINESS.

A sudden stop; a shout; the creaking of an iron gate; the crushing of stones under the wheels as the carriage moved more slowly on.

"We are here."

"Remarkable. I thought we were there. May I take this bandage off my eyes?"

"Not yet," interrupted the stranger, hastily.

The door was opened and Clinton assisted out of the carriage.

Up a short flight of marble steps; across a tessellated porch.

Clinton counted the steps, counted the strides over the porch.

Through a wide door-way into a large hall. Clinton could tell that by the echo of their footfalls.

Up a broad wooden staircase, with massive, carved balustrades.

Clinton did not fail to note every possible particular.

Two wide landings before the upper hall was reached.

Seven paces forward, ten to the right; double doors opened; a large room entered, and the doors closed.

"Stand here a few moments and do not remove the bandage."

The echo of the stranger's steps on the wooden floor was followed by the closing of a door at the other end of the chamber.

Scarcely had the door closed than from the side of the chamber Clinton could hear the noise of another door softly opened and as softly closed.

A gentle rustle of female garments, a low, musical, half suppressed laugh, and all was still.

But Clinton knew that the owner of the garments, the owner of the laugh, was still in the room and not far from him.

He knew it because of a sweet, indescribable, indefinable odor which floated toward him and told him that a delicately nurtured lady was near to him.

He could have sworn she was beautiful. All sorts of visions floated before him. He was almost intoxicated with mystery and imagination.

His first words, however, were characteristic of him, and betrayed none of his real feelings.

"My heart responds to the magic charm of your divine presence. Oh, beautiful and mysterious princess, may I pluck from my eyes these envious folds and gladden my whole soul by the sight of all that grace and beauty?"

"You take too much for granted, monsieur. How know

you I am either princess or beautiful?" came the merry
response in a low, silvery tone.

"That you are beautiful every throb of my heart and
every sense but sight tells me. And you ought to be a
princess, if you are not."

At this moment the door at the other end of the chamber
opened quickly and an angry exclamation followed.

The heavy footfalls of a man approached, and the light
ones of the woman receded.

The two persons met, and a whispered conversation followed.

Clinton strained his ears to catch their words, but was
only rewarded by the question and answer:

"Why such a dress?" from him, impatiently.

"I wish it," from her, defiantly.

"Come, my friends," said Clinton, finally, "don't forget
that I am an eager bridegroom. May I look upon that fairy
form, that heavenly——"

"*Mon Dieu*, my friend," interrupted the man, impatiently, "do have done with such folly. Listen to me.
Have I your promise to comply with whatever conditions we
impose."

"Yes," as long as you keep to your part of the contract.
Now may I gaze as already mentioned?"

"Yes."

Waiting for no second permission, Clinton tore the bandage from his eyes.

A murmur of admiration broke from his lips as he
did so.

He stood at one end of a large saloon, brilliantly lighted
by scores of candles. The furniture was magnificent, in the
massive, antique style. The wainscoting was of dark, time-
stained oak, richly carved.

Clinton knew he was in the chateau of some old and noble
family.

But these details were noticed unconsciously. His eyes
were riveted at once on the figure of the female who stood
in the middle of the saloon, looking toward him.

Her face was covered with a white satin mask.

Her figure was draped in a simple gown of creamy, clinging Japan crape.

Arms and neck were bare, and contrasted a glowing white
against the creamy stuff of the gown.

A dainty, black-slippered foot peeped out from under the hem of the skirt, and the body was slightly bent forward, like Aurora poised for flight.

Such perfection of form, such enchanting grace, Clinton believed he had never seen before.

"Well!" exclaimed she, when, after waiting, Clinton did not speak. "Has the knight of the mysterious adventure lost that glib tongue of his?"

"Faith, no!" answered he, starting from his ecstasy. "But my eyes were so drunk with pleasure as to require all my attention."

"What a pretty compliment!"

"You really are alive, are you?"

"I hope so."

"And you are the bride?"

"I am, indeed."

"Then come to my arms, and——"

"That's not in the agreement," interrupted the man, harshly, and with considerable show of impatience. "If you can restrain your folly long enough, monsieur, we will at once proceed with the ceremony."

"Monsieur," said Clinton, coolly, "are there no windows in this chateau that you presume to use that tone to me? Your hand, mademoiselle. After you, monsieur. We are ready."

With great outward calmness, but burning inwardly with excitement, the artist approached the lovely creature, and taking her by the hand, placed it on his arm with graceful gallantry, and waved the stranger onward.

A moment of hesitation, and the masked man led the way through the side door into a small, square chamber; through that into a hall, and across that into a large octagonal room, so dimly lighted that Clinton could barely see that it was already occupied by three persons—all men, all masked.

CHAPTER IV.

THE INTERVIEW.

"Please put on this white mask."

Clinton did as requested.

"Now let me explain to you. I know that you are a man of honor, and that your promise will be kept."

"You are right," interjected Clinton, earnestly. "Go on!"

The mayor thinks that we have permitted our chateau to be used by a party of romantic Americans for the purpose of celebrating a marriage in a novel way. For this reason he has consented to perform the ceremony in this dark room, and to whisper the names. When the bride's name is about to be uttered, you must place your hand over your ears."

"And after the ceremony, what am I to do?"

"Receive your money, and go back as you came."

"Not even a word with my wife?"

"Not a word."

"Very well," assented Clinton. And then, as the man left him to go out of the room, he whispered to the woman at his side: "And you, mademoiselle, will you not grant a short interview to your husband, who is likely to go mad from too short a glimpse of your divine beauty?"

"Would you really like it?" whispered she.

She was close beside him, and as she looked up and whispered, her breath fanned his face. She seemed to draw nearer to him. Her hand touched his.

A shock ran through him. He was hot and cold in a second. He longed to take her in his arms and rain kisses on the face he knew must be beautiful.

His strong arm was about her waist, and she was nestling, willingly, against him almost before he knew what he was doing.

"Tell me that I may see you again," he whispered in her ear.

"You may," she answered. "Leave it to me. Hush! he is returning."

She drew herself away, letting her hand fall for a moment in his as she did so.

The three men had not observed them.

But Clinton Hastings? Was he in love with this masked woman? Had he forgotten the face in his studio?

In love? Yes—madly, fiercely in love. Forgotten the face? No.

It seemed to him that his soul was in a terrible conflict with the two strange loves.

The face of a woman seen but once—the form of a woman whose face he had never seen.

The woman who was nothing to him—lost. The woman who was to be his wife—lost.

Was he really crazy? Was he bewitched? Where was that reckless coolness of his? Where that mocking spirit?

Gone—all gone.

He would have given his very life that moment only to have held her in his arms and pressed his lips to hers.

The ceremony was gone through with by him mechanically.

He did as he had promised, and closed his ears to her name. Name! What cared he for that? It was herself he wanted.

She was his wife!

The mayor was gone, and he once more stood with his wife and her brothers.

"Monsieur," said the stranger, who had hitherto done all the negotiating, "my brothers will conduct you to the carriage, give you the money as promised, and see you to your home."

"One moment!"

It was his wife who spoke. Clinton listened eagerly, drinking in the sweet tones of her voice, hanging on her every word.

It was his life that hung in the balance.

"Come aside; I wish to say something."

They spoke in low tones, but Clinton heard every word. It seemed to him he could have fathomed their very thoughts, so intent was he.

"You must give me ten minutes alone with him."

"With whom?"

"My husband."

"Are you mad?"

"No, but determined."

"It cannot be."

"It must be."

"Why?"

"I wish it."

"Bah! A woman's reason."

"Be it so; but don't cross me."

"I must, for your own sake and my own. You will ruin us."

"In ten minutes?"

"In one minute. A love-mad woman needs no longer."

"This is folly. I shall go with him to the small square chamber. Prevent it if you can."

"I can."

"Do so, then."

"Come!" she said, speaking aloud to Clinton. "Come with me. I will give you ten minutes."

"Stop!" exclaimed the man, hoarse with passion. "Remember your promise to go as soon as the ceremony was over."

"Oh, Heaven!" murmured Clinton, in agony; for, great as was his infatuation, he would not break his promise. "I did promise," he said, brokenly.

"Aha!" laughed the man. "Did I not know him?"

"Ay," said the woman, tossing her head proudly, "and I honor him the more now that I, too, know him. But you do not know me if you think to outwit me so. If you do not let him go with me, I will go with him. Will you take me, monsieur?"

"Will I?"

"You see," she said, triumphantly, to her brother.

"I see that I may have to use force to make him go without you."

"Dare to touch him, and I speak my name!"

"You would not dare."

"Urge me not too far, or you will know what I dare."

"Woman! woman!" he whispered, fiercely, approaching her, "will you let your mad spirit spoil in a moment our careful plans of a year."

"I tell you I will spoil nothing. Ten minutes! How could I even if I wished. Have I not as much at stake as you? What is it to be? Come, quickly. Shall I speak my name?"

"In Heaven's name, go. Only ten minutes, mind."

"Come, my husband," said she, turning with bewitching grace toward Clinton, and holding out her hand.

No sooner were they out of the room than the four men came hurriedly together and talked earnestly in whispers.

"Now what?" asked the new wife, saucily, as she and Clinton stood alone in the square chamber.

"*Mon Dieu!*" cried Clinton, wildly grasping her two white hands in his. "Must I try to say all that is in my heart in ten minutes?

"Can you not see that I am mad with love—that I will

die without you? Can you not pity me? Tell me that we may meet again. I will search the world on my knees to find you.

"One look at your face, only for a second. Pity me! Pity your slave."

"Clinton," she said, and her voice was low and tender, "I, too, have made a promise. I may not show you my face; I may not give you a clew to my personality; but this much hope I will give you.

"Take this ring. Search for me if you will. If you ever come to me and holding this ring up, say: 'By this ring I claim you for my wife,' I swear to you that I will follow you, though it be to death."

"Now take off your mask, and let me blindfold you."

The infatuated artist kissed the precious ring, kissed again and again the soft hands as they bound his eyes, and then waited for her to speak.

"Will you promise not to move a step or speak a word if I give you something I know you covet, and tell you something I know you long to hear."

"By my love for you I promise it."

"Well, then," the little hands clasped his tenderly, "I love you!"

A cry burst from Clinton's lips.

"Ah! that was wrong. Now," she stood on tiptoe, placed her hands on his two shoulders, and pressed her lips to his.

For one whole minute they stood thus, his arms wound about her pliant figure, her dainty hands upon his shoulders, their lips drinking deep from the fountain of love.

CHAPTER V.

THE ASSASSINATION.

"Where are you, my darling?"

Clinton had awakened from his ecstatic dream of love.

His wife had slipped from his arms and sped away. She was saying to her brother in the other room:

"Now you may have my husband. Treat him well for my sake."

Clinton listening for the slightest sound heard the voice

but could distinguish no words.   The answer of the brother
was more distinct.

"Very well, Madame Hastings, we'll deal with him very
tenderly."

Her musical laugh mingled with the harsher tones of the
four men, who seemed to see a joke in the speech.

"Have you a pillow for him, so he will sleep well," he
could now hear her say, as she apparently followed the men
in the hall.

"Oh, yes, the pillow is provided," was the answer, accom-
panied by another laugh, subdued this time.

Clinton paid no heed to the words then, or to the laugh.
He was conscious only that the woman he so strangely loved
was speaking—speaking of him.

He remembered the words afterward.

The man who had brought him entered the room and ad-
dressed him.

"Are you ready now?"

"I suppose so."

"I leave you now.   My brothers will accompany you on
the journey home."

"Very well."

"You do not ask for your money?"

"I do not want it."

"What?"

"I do not want the money."

"Do not want it; and why, monsieur?"

"Because it is the woman—my wife—I now want."

"You cannot have her, so you might as well take the
money."

"I will not have the money.· I will some day have my
wife."

The man laughed.

"Have your will," he said.   "But at least my part shall
be faithfully performed.   You will be given the money outside.   Throw it away if you will then."

"I will throw it away."

"Come," said a voice new to Clinton—not the voice of a
gentleman.   It was too rough."

Clinton was loth to go, but made no manifestation of any
such feeling.   He had promised.

Down the stairs again and out at the same door he had
entered. Clinton counted his way out as carefully as he had

his way in. He would need such a verification, perhaps, some day."

Not into the carriage did he go, however. He was led along the carriage path, then into a narrower path, and through other paths for a long distance.

The storm the stranger had predicted had come up, and Clinton could not only hear the crashing thunder and feel the heavy rain-drops, but could almost see the vivid lightning through the folds of cloth over his eyes.

He was already much wet when the man who was guiding him suddenly swerved to one side and pulled him into what seemed a sort of arbor.

Clinton could hear the pouring rain on the roof overhead, and could feel earth under his feet.

" Wait here a few minutes," said the man, gruffly, leaving Clinton alone.

" I'm to receive the money here," thought Clinton.

A faint noise behind him caused him to say:

" Bringing me the money?"

" No," came the gruff answer. " It's the pillow your wife sends you."

" Ah!" murmured the artist, tenderly. " Give it to me; I will carry it."

" Take it."

A dull, sickening thud followed, and the blindfolded man fell in a heap to the earth.

Up again he scrambled, tearing the bandage from his eyes.

Half stunned, but desperate; mad with rage and a sense of the black treachery practiced upon him, Clinton grappled with the man.

A low call brought his two fellows, and a silent, terrible death-struggle took place between the four men. Three against one.

*　ʹ　*　　*　　*　　*

The next night a man crept up to the door of the lonely house in Morlaix.

Painfully he ascended the creaking stairs, staggered into the studio, and fell headlong on the floor, clutching at the cloth which hung over the sweet, smiling face.

The painting was uncovered.

The moon shone through the window and fell upon the portrait.

The red lips were curved in a mocking smile, the blue eyes danced with mirth.

The blood-stained face of the man, stern and set, looked up, grim, ghastly.

A black pall fell over the face of the moon.

The lonely house was still.

CHAPTER VI.

THE GARDENER'S ASSISTANT.

Two years later.

The soft, warm sunshine of early spring glanced gayly back from the upper windows of the Chateau d'Iberri. The buds were joyously opening, and the gladsome song of the birds filled the air.

A sturdy young peasant, clad in the picturesque garb of the Breton, walked briskly toward the gates of the chateau.

Over his shoulder, on the end of a stout stick, was a bundle of clothing.

There was no hesitation in the man's air as he walked up to the gates and rapped vigorously on them.

"Good-day to you, Father Pierre," he said, with his rough Breton accent, as a decrepit old man opened a small side-door and looked curiously at the new-comer.

"Good-day to you, lad, whoever you are. I see you are a Breton, or I'd ask for your manners in rapping like that— on the main gates, too!"

"Nay, there, now, Father Pierre! See how lucky I am in coming here, where I can be polished up."

"What mean you by that?"

"Only what you will learn better than I can explain, if you will run your old eyes over this letter."

"Oh," exclaimed the old man, querulously, when he had read the letter. "So you are come to take my place?"

"Nay, now, Father Pierre; I did not so understand it. It seemed to me that I was to assist you. The notary said you had been a faithful servant so long that you deserved more ease in your old age, so I am sent to help you—and that is all."

Somewhat pacified, the old man led the way into his little lodge, and set about finding quarters for the young man, who gave his name as Jacques Bronne.

And so easily satisfied was Jacques, and so respectful withal, that Pierre became quickly reconciled to him.

Indeed, when he reflected that he could now go to the village whenever he liked, his gratification was extreme. He lost no time in testing his opportunities.

"Jacques," said he, "I have important business at the village, and I will start early, for I'm not as supple as I once was."

"Quite right, Father Pierre. I will keep good guard here. If anybody tries to run away with the chateau while you are gone, I'll stop him with this club, which looks as if it had already done good service."

"Nay, Jacques," interposed the old man, hastily. "Never touch that—it has blood on it."

"*Ciel!*" Father Pierre, how comes that?"

"I like not to talk of it, Jacques. I know little, anyhow. Let it suffice for thee that I found it just as thou seest it."

"Ah, good Father Pierre, it is some fearful mystery; I can see that; and you refuse to tell it to me. Ah, you do not know how curious I am, and how I do love a mystery, or you would surely tell me."

"Nay, nay; I will not—at least not now. I must be off!"

"Ah, well," sighed Jacques; "I shall sit here all day, never stirring, with my eyes fixed on that terrible club. It fascinates me."

"A pretty way that to serve your employers," cried the old man, angrily. "Now, I tell thee plainly, thou shalt never hear a word of the story—and it's a rare bloody one—if thou dust not bestir thyself to-day. There's the chateau needs an airing badly. Here are the keys. It's work or no story, young lazybones."

"*Bien*, Father Pierre! If it's that, the work shall not be neglected. I shall have the story to-night, then, eh?"

"Ay, ay. Very well, very well, we shall see," said the old man, good-humoredly, as if talking to a spoiled child. "You'll find plenty to eat in the cupboard."

Jacques watched the old man out of sight, then re-entered the gate and secured it firmly.

The half-stupid, half-joyous look of his class faded from

his face, and gave way to a stern, somber expression. He took up the keys which the old man had pointed out, and then stood a moment looking at the club.

"Ay," he muttered, gloomily; "your story is a rare bloody one, I doubt not; but your turn shall come to-night. Now, to learn what story the chateau can tell."

There was an icy grimness in his manner as he walked along the carriage-drive toward the chateau. He looked neither to one side nor the other, his eyes were on the chateau.

He stood at the foot of the marble stair-way which led from the drive-way to the porch.

What is he doing?

He shuts his eyes, and proceeds to go up the steps. What is he muttering?

"One—two—three—four—five. The same. But wait. One—two—three—four—five—six—seven. Aha! the door. But wait, wait. There may be fifty such. Everything must correspond. Step by step. No jumping to conclusions."

The proper key was found, and the great door was thrown wide open.

Once more closing his eyes, Jacques walked with the same measured step to the staircase, counting, as he went.

"Again the same," he muttered, as his foot struck the lower step. "*Mon Dieu!* I seem to recognize even the very echo. But wait, still wait."

He ascended the stairs, curiously feeling of the balustrade as he went.

"I could swear to this carving. Ah! First landing. Right. Four more—second landing. Now four again. The top. Now seven. So. Half turn to right. Ten. Ah! the door."

"Now stop."

Jacques opened his eyes, and found himself face to face with closed double doors.

"Let me wait a moment. I cannot go in yet."

"What! am I weak? Bah! out upon me. Where is the key? So."

"Open now. And, Chateau d'Iberri, give up your secrets."

With this strange apostrophe Jacques pushed open the doors, and looked in upon a large and lofty saloon. The furniture was worn but magnificent

At the right hand was a door. On the same side near the other end of the saloon was another door. Opposite where he stood was a double door opening into the other end of the saloon.

Coldly Jacques noted all these details.

"It is the same."

Stepping forward a few paces, he stood still and again looked around.

"Ay! I were a fool to doubt it. Nevertheless I will go on to the end."

He opened the door at his right and walked into a small, square chamber.

A half-stifled groan, as if it had but barely escaped the iron grasp of his stern soul, broke from his lips as he entered this apartment.

He scarcely looked about him, and almost quickened that measured pace of his as he passed through it into a hall.

Across the hall he went, and, opening a door, entered a large room of octagonal shape.

"Yes, every detail coincides, and had I not already been sure, my doubts must now have fled.

"There I stood, there she. He there, they there. I can see it as plainly now as then. I hear the voices, subdued and low.

"Oh, Heaven! I cannot go through that night again. Let me hence.

"Not so. I must stay. I must rehearse that scene. Not once, but again and again, until this, the last of all, shall fall like all things else on my flinty heart without calling out one single spark of human emotion.

"Yes, there I, there she, there he. There, there, there. Now the words. So.

"Now to the square chamber."

CHAPTER VII.

THE OATH IN THE SQUARE CHAMBER.

A hard light glistened in the gray eyes of the gardener's assistant as he walked into the square chamber.

But as he stood in the middle of the room it was evident

that an awful struggle for composure was going on beneath the fixed lines of that stern face.

The broad chest heaved with convulsive irregularity, and the nervous hands were clinched in death-like fixity.

A groan at last broke from his lips, white from the close compression.

"Ay!" he muttered. "struggle, man—struggle, devil! Devil have it!

"It was here—this the very spot—that I stood and held her soft white hands in mine. Crazy with the intoxicating love that filled my soul, I could have laid down my life for her with joy. Ay! only sorry that I had not fifty lives to give for as many minutes of the bliss of her presence. She said she loved me."

A faint cry as if he were strangling broke from him.

"At that my heart well-nigh burst with the happiness it could not hold. "Ay! and ay! Every word of it will I recall. Every word, though each one sears my heart as with fire."

The gray eyes blazed with fury, and the lips trembled in agonized writhing.

"'I love you,' she said. 'I love you.' Oh! the music of the words.

"Here, right here, I stood. She there. Her hands on my two shoulders. Oh, Heaven!

"Her bosom pressed to mine, her breath rising to my face like incense to a deity.

"And then in a delirium of love that whirled my whole being into Paradise, I felt her lips against mine.

"Here, right here, she said it. 'I love you.'

"Here, right here, she pressed her lips to mine.

"Ay, let me repeat the words: 'I love you. I love you.'

"Let me remember that kiss! Let me not forget how I loved her then.

"Ah! woman, woman! Better for you had your tongue rotted off at its roots ere those words were spoken, better that vitriol had eaten those lips ere they pressed mine in warm embrace."

A sudden freezing calm succeeded this wild and furious tirade.

Rising to his full height and lifting aloft his right arm in solemn grandeur, he slowly spoke:

"By all the hate of man, by all the false love of woman, by every lying word, by every wicked practice, by that heavenly face and fiendish heart, I swear that no pity will I have, no rest will I take, no other motive shall sway me, in my pursuit of vengeance.

"Sure shall be thy detection, slow shall be thy torture, lingering thy life, horrible thy death.

"As thou hast made me, so will I be."

The head drooped, the uplifted arm fell, and slowly, almost feebly, the man walked from the chamber and made his way out of the chateau.

He leaned against a tree for several minutes, his hand over his eyes.

Slowly the color came back to his set, white face, gradually the robust form straightened.

"The last human emotion is dead," he whispered.

CHAPTER VIII.

THE STORY OF THE CLUB.

"So, Jacques, thou wilt have the story of the club, eh?"

Thus spake old Pierre that night as the two men sat in the little lodge.

"Why, yes, Father Pierre. To speak the truth, there was that in your tone this morning that curdled my blood whenever I did but think of it. I doubt not, Father Pierre. you have the trick of story-telling to a marvel; for I notice you don't forget the little things. Now I love all the small parts of a story, the whys, nows, whereases, and you-should-knows."

"Dost thou, lad? dost thou? Well, now, who knows but it may be as you say," answered the old man, pleased with the flattery. "Though, truth to tell, there's little of this story. Now I could tell thee of the ghosts of Iberri, and I warrant thy blood would indeed run cold."

"Nay, Father Pierre," said the young man, hastily, "the club is in my head, and must be conjured out with thy story."

"'Tis as well it's not *on* thy head, Jacques," chuckled Pierre, "or mayhap thou wouldst be more uneasy."

"Ha! ha! Good! good!" laughed Jacques. "But now to the story, Father Pierre."

"Well, thou must know that ever since the last Marquis
d'Iberri, died, and the estate, without the title, fell into
the hands of a wealthy relative, who cared naught for the
chateau, it has been my custom—with permission, you understand—to let strangers come here and spend a few
hours.

"They were foreigners, mostly, who came. Americans
more than others, for they do say they have only tents and

"SO, JACQUES, THOU WILT HAVE THE STORY OF THE
CLUB, EH?"

mud houses in their country, and of course it pleased them
to see so grand a place.

"I think it was two years ago last fall that a man came
here and asked if he might have the chateau for the night
some time. He wanted to have some joke with a friend,"
he said.

"Was he an American?" asked Jacques.

"American? No. He spoke French as well as thou or
I. Why shouldst thou ask that?"

"Why, you had just spoken of Americans."

"Had I? Well, don't interrupt me, or how can I tell my story right. It was not the usual way of doing, but he gave me a twenty-franc piece, so what could I do but say yes?

"Well, on the night he set he had the old chateau lighted up, particularly the great saloon, and it did make me think of the old times to see it so.

"I don't know what they did, I'm sure. I only know they left about three o'clock in the morning, and I would never have thought of it again but for what happened the next day."

"Ay? What was that?"

"Why, I was walking about the grounds and something led me to an old arbor to the east of the chateau. You may have noticed it. There I saw—what dost thou think?"

"You make me shiver, Father Pierre. Go on."

"Two dead bodies."

"Two!"

"Ay, two."

"And then, what didst thou?"

"What should I do? I reported it to Monsieur the Mayor. He turned as pale as thou art now, and nearly fell from his chair. And no wonder, for it was a frightful thing.

"There was the inquest, and I was a witness and told how the man had used the chateau for the night.

"Then they thought he and his friend had had a falling out and killed each other; but I said nay to that, for neither of the men was he who had seen me. And besides, that man must have gone away in the carriage.

"The jury then decided that the two men were enemies and had gone there to fight it out, and had killed each other.

"But the question was, how had they killed each other, for though they had pistols, they were not discharged.

"Both men were terribly battered, though; so it was evident that they must have had some weapons like a club.

"However, nothing more was thought of the matter until I found this club just under the wall, near the gate, about two weeks later.

"Then I was sure it was what the men had fought with; but the mayor said it was folly, because two men could not kill each other with one club. And so on his advice I said nothing about it, and just kept the club here."

" And you never learned anything more about the matter."

" Not a word."

" Do you know what the name of the man was who used the chateau?"

" Of course not. Why should I ask his name?"

" And no clew to the mystery was ever found?"

" What mystery?"

" How the two men were killed."

" Where was the mystery of that? They killed each other, didn't they?"

" Ah, yes; I forgot that. You don't remember, I suppose, how the man looked?"

" Which one?"

" The one who used the chateau."

" Of course not. Dost thou think I burden my mind with every face I see?"

" Driveling old dotard!" muttered Jacques, under his breath.

" What's that?"

" Did you say there was a lady in the party that night?"

" Jacques, lad, thy wits are wandering. I never said the word lady or woman this night."

" Let me handle the club," said Jacques, getting up and reaching for the gory piece of wood.

" Ha!" he muttered, "lettering on it!"

" What is that?"

" I said it was an ugly club. There, I'll touch it no more."

CHAPTER IX.

THE MARRIAGE REGISTER.

The next day Father Pierre discovered two things, and was both surprised and indignant at the discoveries.

Jacques, his new assistant, was gone, and the bloody club was also gone.

At about the same time that Father Pierre was using bad language in his little lodge, a stranger was being installed in a room in the hotel, in the sleepy little town of Iberri.

He was a tall, dignified old gentleman with heavy snow-white mustache and imperial.

His first care on dismissing the obsequious landlord was to lock the door, and to make sure that he could in no way be suddenly intruded upon.

Then he unbuckled what seemed to be a roll of music in a leather case, and took out what might have been a musical instrument, but was not.

It was a heavy, blood-stained club, bearing a marvelous resemblance to one Father Pierre had lost and was even at that time looking for.

"Now to see what these letters can teach me," muttered the gentleman, closely examining the club.

"T-e-t-e-d-e Fer. Tete de Fer. Iron-head."

Round and round he turned the club, closely scrutinizing it in hope of finding something more, but in vain.

"Iron-head," he repeated over and over again. "Perhaps the nickname of the ruffian, perhaps only a fanciful name for this breaker of human heads less hard than iron. I do not see its value yet, but patience. I have made a good beginning."

No smile of satisfaction lighted up the old gentleman's stern face at this thought. His features were as calm as those of a mask.

"Well, you may wait, old acquaintance," he said, as he returned the club to its case. "I will now call on Monsieur the Mayor, and have a look at the marriage register."

Carefully putting the club in his large valise, the old gentleman went down stairs and asked for the landlord.

Such distinguished looking gentlemen as Monsieur Henri Roche—that was the name signed to the register—so seldom stopped at Iberri, that the landlord hastily abandoned his breakfast in answer to the summons.

"Monsieur will have breakfast, is it not?"

"Why yes, landlord, that is, with two promises. First, to have it quickly; second, to have a bottle of Bordeaux with it."

"As you say, monsieur. Hold, Jean—fetch a bottle——"

"Stop, monsieur landlord; I want good wine, and I know of but one way to be sure of having it.

"How is that, monsieur?"

"By insisting that you shall share the bottle with me. Now order."

"Ah, monsieur," exclaimed the delighted landlord, grinning to his ears. "I shall not order now; I shall fetch it myself."

Seated over the wine, the worthy host was led, with great skill, to discuss the affairs of the town. .

And it was not long before he had told Monsieur Roche that the Mayor of Iberri was a most worthy gentleman who had creditably filled his present post for nearly four years.

After that Monsieur Roche lost interest in his breakfast, and shortly arose to stroll about the town.

He found his way to the city hall, inquired if the mayor was in, and being answered in the affirmative, sent in his card.

The mayor was at his desk, hard at work, and did not look up when his visitor entered. The mayor, be it understood, was too important a personage to stop work for anybody.

The visitor studied the mayor. He saw a man of forty or fifty, small, active, important, avaricious, overbearing.

The mayor continued to write, wondering why his visitor did not speak. The visitor waited calmly for the mayor to stop writing, not neglecting in the meanwhile to carefully note the contents of the room.

"Well, well," began the mayor, at last, in a supercilious tone.

But the moment he looked up and saw the calm dignity of the gentleman before him, his manner changed in an instant.

"Ah, ten thousand pardons, monsieur; have a seat. Really, I thought it was only——"

"Tut—tut, Monsieur the Mayor, do I not know the responsibility that lies on your shoulders? I would not willingly stop one stroke of your pen. Pray finish, and then only will I think of taking up your time with my frivolous errand."

"Oh, monsieur, it is nothing—that is, it can wait. How can I serve you?"

"Well, if you really will not proceed, I will state my errand. I am deputed by the society for the encouragement of marriage, of which, as you know, his majesty the emperor is the president, to obtain statistics on the proportion of marriages to the population in what was the sea province of Britanny. You had been favorably mentioned to the emperor—I do not know by whom—as being the most careful and conscientious officer in the department. Therefore, it was to you I was first instructed to go, in order that I might start right."

So overcome was the mayor by this harangue that he could scarcely more than bow his acknowledgments.

"Monsieur," he managed to say at last, "you do me too much honor, though indeed I have ever striven hard to deserve the good opinion of his majesty."

"And you have gained it, monsieur. Now I will take no more of your valuable time."

"I am only too glad to assist you."

"I believe it; but I can run over some figures if you will permit me to look at some of your books, and when I am through with the mechanical part I will then beg you for your valuable advice. May I first look at the footings in the marriage register?"

"Certainly. Here it is. You will find the footings by years. How far back will you go?"

"Only for ten years."

The mayor's pen scratched. The visitor turned over the leaves of the register.

"Dear, dear!" muttered the visitor, as if under his breath, but in reality purposely loud enough to attract the mayor's attention.

"What is it?"

"Oh, pardon my thoughtless exclamation. It is nothing but a great blot that covers one complete entry."

"Ah—ah, indeed!" stammered the mayor.

"Yes; I can make out only the date. It is November 13, 1865. Fortunately, it makes no difference to me."

"No, no; of course not."

"No; but do you know if I were a criminal officer such a blot as that would make me think?"

"Eh—eh!" gasped the mayor, starting from his chair and looking with blanched face at his visitor.

"Yes."

The visitor laid one hand on the open book and looked placidly thoughtful.

"Yes; because the blot looks intentional."

"Looks in-ten-tional?" faltered the mayor.

"To me, yes.   But I'm afraid you will laugh at me.
Well, I confess I am imaginative.   But do you know I
could fancy that this blotted register means—but I'm afraid
you will laugh at me."

The mayor looked far more like fainting than laughing,
but he contrived to emit a ghostly "he, he."

"Oh, I knew you would laugh."

Monsieur Roche was as calm and frigid as an iceberg.

"However, this is what I could fancy: A midnight marriage."

The mayor gasped and clutched his chair, at the same
time making a horrible attempt to treat the matter as a
joke.

"Masked faces."

Another gasp.

"Whispered responses; hush money for the mayor, who
should carry his register to a deserted chateau."

"*Grand Dieu!*"

The mayor sank a ghastly object in his chair.

"Two men murdered with a club; a fruitless inquest; a
bloody club found and suppressed by the mayor."

"Oh, mercy, mercy, monsieur!   Indeed I am not as
guilty as it seems.   Surely, if you know so much, you must
know that I intended no wrong."

The mayor was groveling abjectly at the feet of his
visitor.

"Will you answer my questions truthfully if I promise
that you shall not be prosecuted?"

"As there is a God above us!"

CHAPTER X.

THE MAYOR'S STORY AND ITS SEQUEL.

"Tell me all you know about the marriage."

"Why, monsieur, the banns were first regularly published at the church."

"There is a record of them, then, giving the names?"

"No, the record was destroyed."

"Ah! and by whom?   But no matter; go on."

"After the banns, a man came to me and said——"

"Was the man a Frenchman?"

"Yes, monsieur, but not a gentleman.   He said that the

lady named in the banns had been living here; that she was going to marry an American gentleman who was so fond of mystery that he wished to be married in masks, as if just from a ball. I said it was foolish, but as I could see no harm in it I consented."

"The whole truth, please. How much did it cost the man to make you think it was not wrong?"

"How quick you are! He gave me five hundred francs. Then he said they wished to be married at the Chateau d'Iberri. I said I could not do that, but——"

"But he argued well; I know. How much for that?"

"One thousand francs. You know about the marriage, perhaps?"

"Yes, you may skip that. Then what?"

"That is all I know. About the dead men I know nothing. I was afraid it might get me in trouble if I said anything, or if anything were learned about them, and that is why I made old Pierre—you know old Pierre?"

"Yes, I know him."

"That is why I told him to keep the stick he found. I will see him and have it destroyed. Had I not better?"

The mayor whined pitifully.

"He has it no longer."

"Who has it, then?"

"I."

"You?"

"Yes. Why not? Who can make a better use of it?"

"About a week after the wedding, some visitors, in looking at the register, made that blot by upsetting the inkstand."

Monsieur Roche looked keenly at the mayor.

"Was the man—perhaps it was a woman, though—who upset the inkstand the same you had negotiated with?"

"No, he was a stranger to me, and—and, to speak the truth, I was not sorry he had done it."

"What did he look like?"

"Indeed, I do not know; for in the hurry and confusion he slipped out of the office, and I did not see him again."

"That is the truth?"

"It is, indeed."

"The only person you really saw was the man who negotiated with you?"

"Yes."

"Describe him. What was his name?"

"I did not know that. He was rather short, heavily built, black eyes and eyebrows, heavy black mustache. He was not a gentleman."

"You mean by that, that he was a ruffian, I suppose."

"I rather suspected it."

"That is all?"

"Yes. No. He had a scar on his forehead, which his hair generally covered; but once I saw it when he accidentally brushed his hair aside.

"He saw me looking at it and laughed.

"I asked him why he laughed.

"He said that scar always made him laugh, for the man who hit him there had intended to kill him, but had not taken into account his iron head."

"*Iron-head!* he said that?"

"Yes, monsieur."

"Can you recall any of the names signed on this register? The blot was well made, and cannot be seen through."

"I can remember one name—that is the first name."

"Ah! What was it?"

"Clinton. I remembered it because it was so odd."

"Bah! And is that all? You cannot recall the woman's name?"

"No."

"And you cannot give me the faintest clew to the names or looks of any of these persons?"

"No, monsieur."

"Good-day, then. I hope for your sake that you have told the truth."

"I have, monsieur. May I respectfully ask if monsieur belongs to the Department of Justice?"

"I do," grimly.

"Ah, then! The partly reassured man became frightened again. "They know it there. I am ruined, ruined."

Monsieur Roche looked contemptuously down at the mayor.

"No. I alone know it."

"And my secret is safe? You will not expose me?"

"Have I not promised?"

"Oh, accept my gratitude! Does monsieur return at once to Paris?"

"Why do you ask?"

"Pardon me. It was only curiosity."

"It was not curiosity; but never mind. Monsieur, the Mayor, listen to me. You love money, do you not?"

"Money is power."

"You love it?"

"Yes, then."

"How much will you take to give me this sheet out of the register?"

"Ah, *mon Dieu!* Money cannot tempt me. I should surely be discovered."

"Very well. I shall talk about you with the lieutenant of police. Good-day."

"Ah, monsieur!"

"Well, then?"

"What will you give?"

"Five thousand francs."

"Say ten thousand."

"Ah! ten thousand. Well, so be it."

"I will turn my back while you take the leaf."

"Not at all. I am not a thief. Bring it to my room at the hotel. I will there give you the money."

"If monsieur pleases, I am afraid it will look ill if I call upon you at the hotel. People may remember afterward."

"You are very cautious. Well, where, then?"

"If monsieur should take the night train away?"

"Yes."

"He might send his baggage, if he have any?"

"Yes."

"To the depot?"

"Yes."

"And meet me at the little bridge north of the depot?"

"Well?"

"Nobody would know then. The transfer could be made quickly, and you could be back in time to take the train."

"Good! I will be there. Do not fail me."

During the day Monsieur Roche tried in vain to get some trace of the record of the banns.

At night he walked through the gloom to the station, left his valise there, and sauntered on to the bridge.

The mayor was waiting for him.

"Have you the sheet?"

"Yes. And you the money?"

"Yes."

"Exchange, then."

The exchange was quickly made.

"I will trust you that the money is right," said the mayor.

"I will not trust you, though, said the other.

And he lighted a match, and quickly glanced over the sheet.

"Is it right?"

"Yes. Good-night."

"Good-night."

The mayor, with an agility not to be expected from him, had barely uttered the words, than he sprang forward and had nearly buried a long, sharp knife in the back of Monsieur Roche.

"Not so, Monsieur the Mayor. I was expecting it."

Monsieur Roche, quickly but calmly, had swung about, and caught the other by the wrist.

A sudden wrench, and the dislocated arm hung limp at the mayor's side. The stiletto fell to the ground.

"Unfaithful officer!" said Monsieur Roche, sternly. "Would-be murderer! Keep the money. It will bring its own curse. Time will punish you. I will take this knife. You will some day see it again."

CHAPTER XI.

TETE-DE-FER.

"Show the gentleman in."

The speaker was a tall, wiry, keen-eyed, soldierly looking personage. He was the Chief of Police in Paris, and knew every rogue in France.

The visitor was announced.

"You are Monsieur Henri Roche?"

"I am."

"You have a letter to me from the Minister of the Interior?"

"Here it is, monsieur."

"You will be good enough to answer whatever questions Monsieur Henri Roche may ask you. He needs information concerning a man who may be known to you. I answer for his discretion. What you do for him will be done for me."

"So, monsieur," said the chief, after reading the letter, "you seek information. Ask."

"I know so little of what I want, that I am afraid you may lose patience with me."

The chief smiled pleasantly, as if his patience was inexhaustible.

"I wish to know if, among the criminals you have record of, there is one known by the name of Tete-de-Fer?"

"Tete-de-Fer?" repeated the chief, reflectively. "That is somehow familiar. Wait! No."

He tapped a bell twice.

"Is the secretary there?"

"Yes, monsieur."

"Ask him to bring here Sobriquet **Book T.**"

"Yes, monsieur."

"I thought," said the chief, "at first that I could fix the man, but I guess it is only a vague recollection I have. You know no other name?"

"No, monsieur."

"Ah, well, here is the book will tell. Names I keep here —faces here."

He tapped his head significantly.

"Ta—Te—Teb—Ted," he read off. "Ah! Tete de— Tete de—bah! Let me look again. No, monsieur, it is not here."

"And there is no other way of finding out?"

"Not unless you had a description of him."

"I have one."

"Ah!"

The chief laid back and shut his eyes to listen.

"Short, thickset, black eyes and eyebrows, heavy black mustache, rough in his manner, a scar on his forehead where a club struck him, scar covered by hair brushed down, voice gruff, speaks with slight Breton accent."

The chief opened his eyes, and smiled intelligently.

Two taps on the bell.

"Francois, bring me Photograph Book No. 57; also Register, letter C. Quickly."

Monsieur Roche's hands closed a little, perhaps, but he made no other sign of emotion.

Francois brought in two large volumes.

The chief turned over the leaves of the photograph book briskly.

"Ah! Look at that!"

Monsieur Roche gazed earnestly at a brutal face, which answered so closely to his description that he had no hesitation in saying:

"It is he!"

"I thought so. Now the description. See, it is almost to a dot like yours, except that this says, 'Nail of little finger of left hand gone.' Now his history:

"'Name, Robert Caradoc; born, 1820; birthplace, Brest, Britanny. Garroter; uses club.' Here follow accounts of his arrests and imprisonments. You don't care for that, I s'pose?"

"No; I want to find him."

"Well, here we have him, I guess. That sort of fellow is seldom long out of prison. Yes, here it is:

"'Attempt at garroting in March, 1866; five years at Toulon.' Eh! 'Escaped; is now in America.'"

A shade may have passed over Monsieur Roche's face, but that was all.

"Nothing more?" he asked, calmly.

"Not a word. If you want him badly, you will have to go to America."

"Yes, I suppose so."

"You will go?"

"I think so."

The chief reflected a moment; then spoke:

"You are a man of judgment. If I could help you, you would ask me, I do not doubt. Still, I offer you my services."

"Thank you. I believe you. You cannot help me now but with advice. How shall I go about finding him in America?"

"Straight to New York. All our rogues go there. Go to the headquarters and look for his picture. If it is not there describe the man to the Chief of Police. I will give you a letter which will open the hearts of the police in New York.

"May I copy this photograph?"

"How?"

"By drawing it."

"Are you an artist, then?"

"Among other things."

"Copy it."

Monsieur Roche took from his pocket a small sketch-book, borrowed a fine pen from the chief, and in a marvelously short time had made a perfect likeness of the man.

"You will find him!" exclaimed the chief.

"Why do you think so?"

"Because you are in earnest. I wish you were one of my agents?"

"What do you mean?"

"That you are beautifully disguised. You took me in completely. If I had not seen your hands, I should never have suspected. But it is all right. I know your introduction is genuine. Some day, tell me who you are."

The chief laughed, pleased to have shown his acuteness.

Monsieur Roche merely bowed.

CHAPTER XII.

THE MARQUIS D'IBERRI.

"Hello! marquis, old fella, ha da dow? Ba Jawve, Ah'm glad to see ya! Ha d'ya like No Yawk? Hah?"

"Well, I yet can zay not egzactly, I am so unaquaint."

"Ha! ha! yas. No, of cawse, ya cawn't. Oh, but, ah saay, marquis, ah'm gone t' introduce ya round, ya know, befaw the season's ova."

"Oh, ah, vralement. I musta egscuse you, buta I can spe'k Engleesh so bad at present."

"Ha! ha! yas, to be sure. Mus' ga roun', ya know, though. Oh, ah saay, Alphonse, jolly glaad t' see ya! Ma friend, Marquis d'Iberri. Marquis, ma friend, Mr. Gorinot. Ya'll be glad to knaw each other. Frenchman in Paris, 'Merican heah. Caame ovah in stimmah togathah, Alphonse."

Mr. Gorinot and the marquis acknowledged the introduction courteously, and the young swell ambled off, feeling that he had done his duty by the dignified young foreigner who had such difficulty with his English.

Two remarkable men they were who stood before each other, gazing earnestly, not to say curiously, at one another.

Both were models in face and figure, but they were as different in type as two men could well be.

The marquis was tall and muscular. His clean-shaven

face was rather Saxon than French in style, and was peculiar for the firm set of the lower jaw, and the calm, penetrating expression of his gray eyes.

There was a fascinating grace in his manner, and a seductive charm in his melodious voice; but the dignity of his bearing almost chilled.

Alphonse Gorinot was almost what the marquis was not. Short, slight, active, but not muscular. His dark-skinned oval face set off by dark-brown mustache and imperial.

The eyes vivacious, but not confidence-inspiring; the mouth mobile, but, in repose, almost cruel.

"Where have I seen him before?" the marquis asked himself.

"I can claim you as countryman, marquis," said Gorinot, in perfect French.

"Your French proves that. But how is it?"

"Why, my parents were both French, and I was partially educated. in France. My father died, my mother married an American, and I came here. I keep up my French by going over regularly. I wonder I never met you in Paris."

"I seldom am there, and, except to attend the emperor's receptions when I must, I do not go out at all. But for all that, I can't help thinking I have seen you."

"Very likely," laughed Gorinot. "I don't hide my light when I'm in Paris. But look here; you must be awfully bored in this city, with nobody but waiters to speak your own language to. Come take dinner with us to-night, and go to the opera. We all speak French at our house."

"Really you must excuse me."

"No, I won't. What! a real, live marquis to be allowed to vegetate in New York! You don't know the people. Take my advice and come with me. If you don't, you'll be run to death with tuft-hunters. That young Jones will make it the business of his life to introduce you around. Ba Jawve."

Gorinot laughed merrily, and then went on:

"You don't believe me. All right. See, there's Jones now, bringing two worshipers to your shrine."

The marquis could not doubt it, for there was the eager young swell, arm in arm with two acquaintances, making straight toward them.

"Come," said Gorinot. "Let's escape."

They walked into the reading-room of the hotel in which the scene had taken place.

"Now, marquis," went on Gorinot, in his volatile way, "you see how it is. You'd better surrender gracefully. We're used to titles at our house, and won't persecute you."

"Not to make it quite a surrender," answered the marquis, pleasantly, "let me say that I accept with pleasure."

"That's right; and when I meet you in Paris you can show me the lions there."

"I'm afraid you know them better than I do."

"Well, then, I'll show them to you."

That evening a carriage drove up to a stately mansion on Madison avenue, and the marquis got out.

"Ah, marquis, you did not play me false, then. And well for me that you did not, for the ladies are crazy to have a new man to talk French with. They are tired of me."

Gorinot led the marquis into the drawing-room.

"Marquis d'Iberri, my aunt, Mrs. Howard, my sister, Miss Howard. Eh! Why, marquis, are you ill?"

"No, no, a mere trifle—a spasm—quite gone now."

Gone it did seem to be, but a trifle it surely was not, for the marquis was not the man to change color to a ghastly white, put his hand on his heart, and moan for a trifle.

Gone like a flash it was, and the marquis was his cool, dignified self in an instant.

"Pardon me, ladies. Put it down to my pleasure in meeting ladies with whom I can exchange thoughts in my own language."

"Oh, Heaven!" he was saying to himself, "why was I led here? Why have I seen that face again?"

What face?

Was it that of Grace Howard?

If so, why should a face like hers make him turn pale? A fairer face never was looked upon.

A little of melancholy in it, much womanly sweetness, much maidenly archness. Much that was tender, much that was honest and true.

Ravishing beauty, bewitching grace.

Limpid, soulful blue eyes, moist, tempting, cherry lips.

Freshness and health on the peachy cheeks. Teeth of ivory; dimples for Cupid himself to envy.

The vivacity, frankness, joyousness of a girl, the dignity and self-possession of a woman.

CHAPTER XIII.

THE PORTRAIT OF THE LONELY HOUSE.

No one would have recognized the vindictive Jacques Broune, the cold, hard Henri Roche, nor even the dignified, distant Marquis d'Iberri in the entertaining young Frenchman who joyously basked in the sunshine of Grace Howard's presence that night.

All the hauteur and freezing courtesy of the marquis had melted away before the charm of the beautiful young woman's companionship.

In the manner of the marquis was much of the lightsomeness and manly grace of Clinton Hastings, though with none of the artist's reckless humor.

During all the evening nothing but happy thoughts found a place in the handsome young Frenchman's mind.

It was wonderful to see how the stern intensity of his clear gray eyes faded away and gave place to a reflection of the frank gayety which lighted up the deep blue eyes of sweet Grace Howard.

And the fixed lines of his mouth were gone; and the lips that an hour before looked as if they were made to utter death-sentences, now curled with many a merry jest or parted in light laughter.

Fascinated and completely carried away the marquis lived only for the moment.

If a thought of the wonderful change, so suddenly come over him, entered his mind he cast it out with all the gay thoughtlessness of reckless Clinton Hastings.

When others listened to the music and looked upon the performers on the stage he gazed only at her and drank in great draughts of love.

"It is fate," he said to himself, "sweet fate that has brought this about. And I was chiding fate for it! Ah, Clinton, Clinton, you little thought when you spent all those hungry days gazing at her inanimate picture that Heaven would ever be as kind to you as this.

"Why is it that I loved her so when love was hopeless—mad, unless fate urged me on.

"Why should I meet her now a free woman to hear my love if fate had not so willed it?

"Why, after my terrible sufferings and the hardening of my soul, should I meet her now, a sweet angel to pour balm upon my heart wounds if fate had not willed it?

"In love with another? It may be, but I do not believe it, for in those deep blue eyes when I looked in them came up the reflection of a free maidenly heart.

"Oh, I will win her, I will win her. I must. I will let her see into my heart and read its earnestness and passion.

"It cannot be that fate has led us together only to mock at me.

"She shall be mine, and I will make her so happy—happy as only such an angel of purity as she deserves to be."

And as the short hours sped away they carried with them the sweetest moments of Clinton Hastings' life.

Deeper and deeper he drank from the fountain of love, and his whole being was in a strange ecstasy of bliss.

How marvelous was it that a strong, iron-willed man could thus be carried away by a sentiment born in a moment of a chance glimpse of a sweet face, and strenghtened into an overpowering vitality by one short evening of companionship!

When Clinton Hastings, or Marquis d'Iberri—for he was lawfully both—reached his room that night, he gave himself over to the sweet joy of hope.

Gone was every hard thought from his heart; fled was the spirit of vengeance; forgotten the fearful oath of the square chamber.

"Bah!" he exclaimed in disgust. "I was going to make a hangman of myself, and gloat over the sufferings of a woman who had played with my heart, and then tossed me to death like a piece of carrion. What care I for her or what she did, now that I may win my first and true love! That was a wild infatuation for the masked creature, though, and she was superb. Good Heaven! when I think of her perfidy, I——. No, no, Clinton, don't think of it. You were to blame, too. You led her on to play with you by giving way to that insane burst of passion. No, no, let her go."

But, ah! what terrible thought is this that starts him to his feet, the cold beads of perspiration standing thick on his forehead!

What could tear that groan from his throat?

"But, oh, good Heaven! good Heaven? I cannot let her go! I must hold to her as she has to me. We are bound! Oh, why did I forget that? Why did I not remember that in time? Must my heart go back to its prison? my soul shrink back into its nothingness, after the bliss, the freedom of this night! Oh, Heaven! Is there a fate in this? Must that angel face be ever a forerunner of the hand that shall score its bloody tracks upon my heart!"

The young man stopped; a storm of rage contorted his mobile features; the left hand pressed upon his breast, as if to still the beating of his heart.

The struggle was short; the convulsed features resumed their repose.

Not the joyous repose of the evening, but the fixed repose of the afternoon. A baleful light was in the gray eyes.

"Is it perdition that drives me?"

His voice was hoarse."

"Well, and why not? What matters it, anyhow? It is enough I am driven. There stand the gates of Paradise open to me, but I must pass through perdition to reach them. I come. Woman, beware. When vengeance alone spurred me on, I was terrible. Now, vengeance is but an instrument, and no demon could be more merciless than I in using it!"

CHAPTER XIV.

THE MAN WHO KILLS WITH A CLUB.

The next day, when Alphonse Gorinot called to see his new friend, the marquis, he was surprised to receive a note from that young gentleman, saying he had been called away on business of importance, but would return before long to continue an acquaintance so happily begun.

The same day, Henri Roche, impassible, grave, and stern as ever, took rooms at a quiet hotel down town.

A little later he called at the Police Headquarters, and,

after handing over his letters, was invited to the sanctum.

The chief received him courteously, at the same time studying him with the quick glance of an expert in physiognomy.

Nothing did he make of Henri Roche, however.

" You are looking for a criminal, then, eh?"

" Yes, sir."

" He is wanted on the other side?"

" No; or, at any rate, I am not on that mission. I only want to extract some information from him."

" Let me see his description."

It was handed to him.

" I don't recognize him, and I guess he hasn't passed through my hands yet. But, I tell you—you just run your eye over those photographs, and I'll send for a detective who keeps track of all our foreign visitors."

Roche did as directed, but he saw no face in the ugly assortment at all like the one he was in search of.

The detective came, studied the description, and was silent a few moments.

Henri was impassive.

" I won't swear to the man from this," said the detective, at last; " but if you'll go with me, I'll point out the man I think fits it."

" Perhaps this picture will help you.

" That's the man," said the detective at once. I can lay my finger on him at any time. What is it—extradition?"

" No. He knows something I want to know."

" Sorry for that. Chief, he's the chap they call Frenchy. He's suspected on that bank job, you know; but we haven't fixed it yet. I'd like to lay hands on him, too; for I'm dead certain he's the one who downed poor Bill Curtis. Don't you know Bill had his skull broke the same way as the bank janitor?"

" Yes, yes, I recollect. Perhaps, Dan, you and this gentleman could work it together some way to get the drop on him. What do you think, sir?"

" I think it is a good idea."

Roche and Dan Hartley had a long and earnest conference together, the gist of which was all contained in the few final words of summing up.

" Then it's this way," said Dan; " you're to join 'em and get Frenchy's confidence. Of course you speak French?"

"Like a Frenchman—as I am."

"Pshaw! I took you for English. Well, if you can get good evidence against him, without appearing yourself, on the old bank job, or anything else, I'll fall on him. If you can't, get into some job with him, give it away to me, and I'll see it through. After we've got him you can use him any way you please."

"Good. Now give me a password, so you'll know me in my disguise."

"Oh, I guess I'll know you."

Dan smiled at the idea of a password.

"Perhaps; but to be sure, let's say 'Vengeance.'"

"All right. 'Vengeance' then. And I don't know but you're right, for I may have to fix up, and you'll want some way to know me."

Henri Roche smiled now.

The two men took a keen look at each other, and each divining what the other's purpose was, they both smiled and shook hands cordially.

CHAPTER XV.

THE IRON-ARM AND THE IRON-HEAD.

About two hours later, a heavy, brutal-looking man of about twenty-five, a foreigner, and apparently a stranger in the city, turned from Canal street into Mott street and walked carelessly down it, looking carefully along both sides of the street.

He was fairly well dressed, and wore not a little jewelry; but the brutality of his face could not be overcome by any such means, and in spite of an effort to leer pleasantly at some passing woman, he was forbidding in the extreme.

Apparently he did not find what he wanted, for he stopped and turned back, hesitated, and looked up and down the street in great perplexity.

A vegetable huckster was passing—he hailed him.

"Looka! I wanta hotel Italiano. He tella me een disa strit."

"I don't know enny sech hotel. Ax some o' those fellers hanging round that saloon."

"You can aska him."

"What would I ask for? Ask yourself. Got a tongue, ain't ye?"

And the huckster hurried off, apparently anxious to escape any more talk with the fierce Italian.

"Vengeance!" whispered the foreigner.

"Sold!" exclaimed the huckster. "You'll do!"

Henri Roche, or Jean Lenoir, as he now called himself, having given Dan Hartley a sample of his ability, put aside his Italian accent, and assuming that of a southern Frenchman, walked into a little French eating-house and called for a bottle of wine.

The eating-house was, in fact, the rendezvous of the particular gang of desperadoes to which Robert Caradoc, or Frenchy, belonged.

That is, Frenchy consorted with his outcast countrymen there, but he did not do business with them.

Most of them were on a different lay from his, and, moreover, he had learned caution by experience at home, and kept away, when he was not working, from his business associates.

He and some of his friends were playing vingt-et-un at a table at the farther end of the room.

They were not so fully engaged, however, that they did not see the new-comer, and note his jewelry.

They also noted his style, and they were satisfied that he was not their game.

When Jean had finished as much of the wine as he could drink, he walked ever to the table and looked on at the game, taking such a position as would enable him to get a good look at Caradoc.

"Take a hand?" inquired that worthy, in choice French slang, or "argot," as it is called in Paris.

"I don't care if I do," replied Jean, in the same dialect. "I like to play with friends."

"What lay are you on?" quietly inquired one of the men.

"I'm a banker, well known in Paris. The weather is warm there just now, and I left for my health."

A coarse laugh greeted this sally, and the game went on, until one of the men who was losing became angry, and thinking the new-comer a good subject for his ill-temper, opened on him, and accused him of cheating.

"You're a liar," said Jean, coolly.

Without any waste of words the man, who was a burly fellow, whipped out his knife and sprang at Jean.

The others moved aside to watch the fun in safety.

Jean caught the man, took the knife from him as if he had been a child, and drove it to its hilt in the table.

"Don't be a fool," he said, "or I'll dislocate your arm. It's a trick I have."

With an oath the man rushed at him again, unable to believe that he could have been so easily worsted, except by a trick he could overcome.

Jean caught him, whirled him about, took him by the arm, and threw him away with a peculiar twist.

The man's right arm hung limp—dislocated.

"I told you so," said Jean, quietly. "This is my trick. They call me Bras-de-Fer (Iron-Arm) in Paris."

"Aha," laughed Caradoc, glancing admiringly at him, "we must be related then, for I have been called Tete-de-Fer."

"Bravo, comrade!" exclaimed Jean; "let's have a bottle to better acquaintance. That is, if the old villain here has anything but the sour poison he just gave me. I guess he thought I was an Italian."

Then turning to the man who was groaning with pain, he said:

"Look you, *mon ami*, I bear you no ill-will, and if you are satisfied I will throw your arm back and you shall drink with us. What say you?"

"Eh, *mon Dieu*, Monsieur Bras-de-Fer. Yes, I am satisfied, and I hope you are."

"Oh, yes, I needed some sort of introduction to you all, and I guess this will do. Eh?"

He looked around inquiringly.

"Yes, yes," was the admiring affirmative.

A skillful pull and turn sent the dislocated arm back in its socket with a snap.

"Now rub that with liniment to-night, and in a week you will be all right, unless you should call me a cheat again."

There was no trouble after that in entering into the most cordial relations with all the men excepting Frenchy.

Frenchy admired and respected the man who was so strong, and who bore him so masterfully.

But Frenchy saw no reason why he should take him into his confidence until it should be profitable to do so.

Consequently Jean played cards and drank bad wine with his wily compatriot to no avail, until he saw that he must be the one to propose a scheme.

"*Mon ami,*" said he. "It seems to me an iron head and an iron arm could do good work together."

"How?" inquired Frenchy, cautiously.

"Come to my room."

Frenchy followed him.

"I told you I was a banker in Paris."

"Yes."

"Well, I am interested in banks here, then, of course."

Frenchy laughed.

"For a week I have been studying the system of one of the banks here."

"Did you learn much?"

"Not as much as I wanted to, and so I wanted you to help me."

"How can I?"

"I don't speak English well yet, and the janitor might not understand me. You could interpret."

"Is that all?"

"That's all. We will go around there some pleasant evening when the moon is not too bright. You will tell the janitor something for me, and then we will come away."

"What shall I tell him?"

"Tell him that if he makes any noise you will phlebotomize him."

"Phlebotomize? What is that?"

"That means to open a vein and let out a little blood. It is a medical term."

"You are learned."

"Yes, I once assisted a doctor to bank his money."

Frenchy laughed. He was delighted with Bras-de-Fer.

"And when I tell him that, what will you do?" he asked.

"I will go down stairs and make a final study of the banking system."

"What bank is it?"

Jean described where the bank was.

Frenchy pursed his lips and shook his head. He did not think much of the sagacity of Bras-de-Fer.

"Why," said he, "the safe is right where anybody passing can see it."

"Certainly, that is the kind I prefer. It is the easiest."

Frenchy looked surprised and incredulous.

"Ah, I see," said Jean. "You are not learned, as you have said I am. Now look."

He took down a square mirror from the wall and placed it behind one of the legs of the table.

Any person looking, would have thought he saw both front and hind legs, when really it was only the front legs reflected.

"Now do you understand?"

Frenchy shook his head. He was mystified.

"Well, suppose I wanted to work behind that table, and did not want to be seen, and did not want anybody to know that the table was being used as a screen; if I put a large mirror behind the two fore legs but in front of the two hind ones, would not anybody suppose he could see right under the table as well as usual?

"Of course; but is there a table in front of the safe?"

"Yes."

"And a mirror large enough?"

"Yes."

"*Mon ami*, I will also study the banking system."

And Tete-de-Fer laughed heartily at his own joke.

"You will be as learned as I 'some day'," said Bras-de-Fer.

CHAPTER XVI.

FRENCHY STUDIES THE BANKING SYSTEM.

"Now," said Jean, as he and Frenchy walked along together one suitable night, "after you have gagged and tied the janitor, just take a look in his coat-pocket, for I saw him receive a roll of bills this afternoon."

"I'll not forget."

"But don't phlebotomize unless you must. It's no use to make him feel any more than is necessary. I'm very tender-hearted, you see.

Frenchy laughed.

"Here we are. Quick now, after me!"

Jean with a key opened the side door and vanished inside, followed by Frenchy.

"Now go up, and when you have fixed the old man and got his money, give three taps on the baluster. If you don't get the money, give one tap on the baluster and two taps on his head."

Frenchy crept up stairs to the janitor's room and performed his work there very creditably.

But while he was doing so Jean slipped out into the street, and four men went quietly up stairs.

In a short time Frenchy came out of the room and tapped three times on the baluster.

A short scuffle, and Frenchy, securely handcuffed, was led to the station-house.

Frenchy had a good lawyer, but, unfortunately, had been too successful in the janitor's room, and therefore, in default of any political friends, he was sentenced for ten years.

This gave him ample time to study the banking system. He had not turned his attention to that study yet, however, when he was visited in his cell by a tall, dignified old Frenchman.

"Henri Roche is my name. Do you know me? Look well."

Frenchy looked sullenly up and answered gruffly:

"No, I don't know you."

"Well, Tete-de-Fer, Robert Caradoc, native of Brittany, I know you."

"Much good may it do you."

"It may do me good. We shall see. Would you like a voyage to England or South America? In fact, would you like to be free?"

"Does a cat love milk?"

"You can go free if you will answer some questions I will ask."

"Better set me free first and ask afterward."

"Not such a fool as that."

"All right ; then I don't talk."

"Oh, yes, you will."

"Will I? We'll see."

"Suppose I could prove two or three murders of yours?"

"Suppose you could?"

Frenchy could not prevent a little pallor coming to his face, though he did try to talk bravely.

"I can. Do you remember the young American at Chateau d'Iberri?"

"I didn't kill him. He got away."

"How far away?"

"I don't know. He killed my two pals, stunned me, and got away. He was a devil."

"WELL, TETE-DE-FER, ROBERT CARADOC, NATIVE OF BRITANNY, I KNOW YOU."

"Well, he was found dead on the road the next day."

"I'm glad of that."

"Are you? Well, you can hang for it. Also the detective you killed. Will you talk?"

"What do you want?"

"Well, now, listen. You know something I am willing to pay for in money, and set you free, too. I can do it. I got you in here, and I can get you out."

Monsieur Roche assumed the tones of Bras-de-Fer.

"Say, ami Tete-de-Fer, are you yet learned in the banking system?"

"*Mon Dieu*, a detective!"

"Exactly."

"If I answer you will have me set free?"

"I will."

"Go on."

"How came you to be engaged in that Chateau d'Iberri affair?"

"Very simple. I was hired."

"Who hired you?"

"I don't know."

"Don't know?"

"No; I never saw him without a mask."

"How much were you paid?"

"Ten thousand francs."

"Just to kill the young man?"

"Oh, no; I was to drive and sign my name as witness to the marriage."

"Tell me about the murder. How was it planned?"

"At first I was to drive him part way home, pretend an accident, have him get out, and break his skull. But the young fellow and his sister got the idea that the American suspected something, so he got her to entice him into another room for a few minutes while we fixed it for a new plan."

The bands of Henri Roche closed tightly.

"We were to lead him into the garden and do him there. Any other man would have given in, but he was a devil. How he did fight!"

"Are you sure the woman knew of the plan to murder the American?"

"Know it? Of course she did. Why, I can hear her now saying, so sweet-like, 'Have you the pillow for him?' meaning my club. *Mon Dieu!* yes, she and her brother had it all planned."

"And you do not know anything about either of them, their names or looks? Think. Five thousand francs for a clew of some sort."

"I could never see his face nor hers, nor hear their names, though I tried hard, too. But wait. I did find his handkerchief—a silk one."

" Find it?"

" Yes; found it in his pocket.   It had his initials on."

" Ah!   What were they?"

" That is what I don't remember."

" And the handkerchief?"

" That I gave my sister."

" And do you think she has it still?"

" Quite likely."

" Where is she?"

" In Paris."

" Where?   What street?"

" That cannot matter to you."

" It does matter, for I must have that handkerchief."

" But look you, monsieur.   I have my own reasons for keeping that secret.   I will send to her and have her send it to me.   You can leave me here till the answer comes. Only if she has lost it you must not hold me accountable."

" Well.   But I warn you—no trifling.   You know Bras-de-Fer, but you don't know me."

" I will be faithful, you may be certain.   I'd rather have five thousand francs than a silk handkerchief."

" Let this be the agreement, then.   The day you send me word that you have the handkerchief I will have you set free and give you fifteen thousand francs."

" Good.   But if I cannot get the handkerchief?"

" If you honestly can't—and I will make myself sure of that—you shall go free.   No money, though."

" And where shall I send word?"

" Suppose I come here in two months?   Will that be time?"

" I think so."

" Good.   In two months then.   And do not forget this: I have long arms, and can reach far.   If you play me any trick, I will so do to you that you will curse the hour you were born."

Frenchy believed Monsieur Roche.

CHAPTER XVII.

HIS FIRST AND OWN TRUE LOVE.

Had the acquaintances of the Marquis d'Iberri forgotten him? He was not a man to forget.

Alphonse had almost daily looked for his return, until the family joined in the usual summer flight from town, when he went too, and gave up hope of ever seeing him again in America.

He did not know the magnet that drew the marquis, or he would not have despaired.

The summer was still young when the marquis arrived at the gay watering-place where the Howards were sojourning.

He was at the same hotel.

The first morning he sat in his room, talking to himself.

"Yes, I am here. I could not stay away. I have two months of respite, and for that time I will be human. After that if I am fortunate—bah, how can I be? Only a handkerchief."

"Well, never mind what comes then; for these two months, come what will, I shall be happy. Only I must beware that my tongue betray not my heart."

"Ah! I wonder if she even remembers me?"

"Why, marquis, is it indeed you? We had thought you were not pleased with America and had hurried back to France."

Frankly the little hand was put in his, honestly the blue eyes looked into his gray ones, gayly the cherry lips smiled over the white teeth.

If a blush or two played hide-and-seek on her soft, round cheeks when she searched the depths of his speaking eyes, why it was not the marquis who was going to find fault.

"America!" he exclaimed. "Truly, that first night I did not know I was in it. I thought I had made a mistake and fallen into Paradise."

"Oh, fie! Marquis, such compliments do not please me. Save them for somebody else."

"Pardon me. It was not intended as a compliment. I was betrayed into telling what I really felt."

"There, there! that's no better—worse, rather. Now let us talk of something sensible. What have you been doing?"

"What! talk of me? Do you call that a sensible topic? Nay; let us talk of something beautiful. How have you been?"

"I shall speak English, if you will persist."

"I do believe you could make even English sound sweet."

"At the next speech like that I shall run."

"Don't do that; and if you will not believe in my sincerity, lay it to the fact that I have lost my wits in the pelasure of seeing you again."

"Will you find them if I leave you?"

"Indeed, no. It is only by being near you that I can save them."

It is folly to repeat the words of lovers; so let them be untold.

But were they lovers?

Everybody said so. Alphonse took it for granted, called on the Marquis d'Iberri, and borrowed money of him.

The marquis knew he was in love. He knew he lived in it. He knew she did not repel him.

Was she in love? Well, she was melancholy when he was not by her side, and she was a picture of happiness when he was.

When she saw him coming her eyes lifted up and a glad smile played on her sweet mouth.

Perhaps she thought he did not love her.

Perhaps she did not know that he worshiped her.

Perhaps she wondered that he did not, in so many words, say "I love you."

Possibly he was in doubt about her feeling for him.

Possibly he did not suspect that he was her ideal of manhood.

Possibly it was not on his tongue's end fifty times a day to say "I love you."

Perhaps, and possibly.

Mrs. Howard was satisfied, Alphonse was satisfied.

The truth was, Grace was not to be interfered with; and had any word been spoken by anybody about the relationship of the marquis to her, it would have been discovered that she could be trusted to take care of herself.

The love was understood, but not spoken.

CHAPTER XVIII.

WHEN THE FLOOD-GATES OF LOVE WERE OPENED.

As the happy weeks flew by, and the time narrowed down to within a few days of when the marquis must keep his appointment with Tete-de-Fer, the young man became restless, and totally unlike his well-contained self.

It was useless for him to evade the issue before him.

He might, indeed, declare his love, and make Grace his wife, for he was confident that she would consent.

He knew the masked woman could never recognize him, even if she dared to avow herself.

Nevertheless, he could not for one moment contemplate the thought of deceiving the pure, confiding Grace.

How two such conflicting sentiments as his love and his bitter hate could find room in the same breast, would have been impossible to comprehend, were it not for the fact that it was only by the satisfaction of his vengeful hate that he could dare to indulge in his love.

Hours he spent in the darkness and solitude of his chamber, wrestling with his fate.

Could he leave Grace, and devote months, or years, maybe, to the pursuit of vengeance, without saying to her one word of love?

Could he tell her the truth, and ask her to wait for him?

Tell that innocent, gentle girl of all the treachery, blood, and hate in which he had been an actor!

Tell her that he would have her wait for him until he could compass the death of a woman!

What then?

"Deceive her, or tell her?

Speak his love, or leave it unspoken?"

To leave it unspoken would now be dishonorable.

To speak it when he was bound to another woman would be even worse.

Why not give her up? Why not tear loose from this great love which so enthralled him?

Give her up?

The very thought made him turn with savage fury to the picture of the vile creature who could plot his murder, and in the same instant lavish on him such kisses and caresses as melted his very soul into hers.

And yet, even then, he loved this sweet Grace of his. Even then he was as much her mad worshiper as now.

Was he unlike other men, that he should start from his dream of love for an angel of purity, and fling himself, with hot words and passionate impulse, into the arms of the first seductive siren who crooked her finger at him?

Was this love that was in him, or was it insanity?

"Great Heaven?" he exclaimed; "what is it? What am I? Who was she? Whence this sudden power over me?"

Over and over he trod the same ground.

At one moment his gray eyes were blazing with the fires of hate; at another melting with love's soft light.

One by one the days went by, stopping neither for his love nor his hate.

And as each day passed, and another came, Clinton wondered he was not mad.

And each morning, as jaded and weary, he found himself irresistibly drawn toward the object of his love, he would say to himself:

"This shall be the last time. To-morrow I will go."

And the moment her soft blue eyes searched his; the moment her sweet voice bade him welcome; the moment her little hand rested confidingly in his, that moment he was lost to everything but her love and his.

Was his love?

Well, be it love or madness, it controlled him, strong-willed man as he was, as if he had been a nerveless child.

Three days he had yet.

And Clinton, at midnight, after one of his terrible battles with himself, sat, asking himself:

"What shall I do then? To-morrow, and the next day, and the next. Shall I be dead? Shall I be chained up in a mad-house, a raving maniac? Shall I dishonor myself and her by asking her to be my wife? My wife! oh, hideous mockery! My leman! Woman! fiend! I could tear you limb from limb, had I you in my clutches!"

"Fire! fire!" came a sudden, hoarse cry.

Clinton shook himself, as if to throw off the sea of passion in which he had been plunged.

More cries, and a confused sound of hurrying feet.

Clinton listened.

Probably the hotel was on fire.

"Well," he smiled, grimly, "fate points the way. Let the fire come. I will wait for it."

He sat down by the window, and calmly looked out.

The red flames must have already burst out. Clinton could see crowds of people, in night raiment, hurrying to and fro on the lawn in front.

There seemed to be few or no facilities for meeting the fire-fiend.

Every man giving vain orders, every woman and child screaming.

Mothers crying for children, given in charge of hired nurses; children crying for nurses.

Panic and confusion.

Clinton smiled bitterly, and never moved. Then a tender thought filled his heart.

"Ah, Grace, my darling! You will never know that my last thoughts were of you. Would I could have lived to make you happy! But that may not be. Fate has otherwise ordained. My blessing be with you, and may you live——. Ah! but will she live? Great Heaven! she, too, is in danger! Dog that you are! Besotted in self! Calmly talking of dying when she may be in all the agonies of fear and danger!"

It may be believed that Clinton did not sit still and deliver this apostrophe to himself.

The moment the thought of danger came to him, he sprang from his seat, and plunged down stairs.

Through flames, smoke, and burning timbers, he rushed.

He knew her rooms well. He must first go out in order to reach them.

Out he darted into the night air; into the pandemonium there.

Nothing of this did he see or feel.

Fiercely on he flew to the stair-way leading to her rooms.

"Ah, D'Iberri! have you seen Grace?"

It was Alphonse.

"No."

Clinton threw him off as if he had been a fly.

Grace was in danger, then. She was not with her brother.

The flames were bursting forth at the very door he must enter.

"I can die with her, at least."

He dashed toward the door.

A crowd of men tried to bar his way.

"Out!" he cried, with a howl like a madman.

The men were flung off like children.

Into the flames, and through them.

Up the burning stairs, the charred and blazing steps breaking under his feet.

Through the winding corridors, half-choked with thick smoke.

Up another flight.

Around, and up again.

"She must be safe yet," he muttered. "The fire is mostly down stairs."

At her room door at last.

The door fell in like a sheet of paper before his mighty strength.

But just arisen, still in her night-robes, Grace stood before him, the wild firelight showing her great blue eyes filled with half-wonderment, half-fear.

"Grace, my own darling! It is not too late then!"

A sweet smile broke upon her lips.

She looked like a little child, or like an angel from heaven, as she stood in the midst of all that horrid danger, in her pure white robe, and with that smile of joy and confidence on her face.

"The hotel is on fire?" she queried.

"Yes."

Clinton answered shortly, for he was busied in saturating with water a blanket which he had snatched from the foot of the bed.

He wound it about her, covering even her head and face. There was no time for explanation. None was needed; she yielded herself to him with a composure and a confidence that even then filled him with a fierce joy.

She could trust him so much then.

He would have marveled at her composure, had he not rejoiced in it.

She was no weight for his strong arms, but he trembled as he took the precious burden up.

Out again, swiftly but carefully.

The devouring flames had crept up after him, and were even now thrusting their forked tongues through the boards of the corridor.

The whole of the lower part of the house was a blazing mass; the stairs had fallen in.

The roof was the only refuge.

Up, up he climbed.

Instinct seemed to tell him where the roof ladder was.

Once on the roof he looked about him.

The flames were nowhere visible.

If he could but reach the edge! He knew the main building was flanked by wings with lower roofs.

They might not yet have caught fire.

He dragged the ladder after him.

He pulled aside the blanket from Grace's face to give her fresh air.

"Courage, darling! We may yet be safe. You trust me?"

She smiled.

"In life or death."

Clinton groaned.

Must such love as this, with all its future of bliss, be lost!

Grace clasped tightly to his breast by one strong arm, the ladder lightly carried in the other hand, Clinton sped toward the right wing.

"Oh, Heaven!"

Almost under his feet the roof collapsed, fell in, and was ingulfed in the yawning abyss of flame.

Back he turned.

Ah! would he reach the other end in safety?

Was that a red tongue of flame?

"Heaven!" he moaned.

"I cannot die now. I will not!"

Almost there!

Crash!

Fifty feet of leaping flame between him and the towering wall beyond.

Behind him flames! Before him flames! On either side sixty feet to the ground!

"Grace, darling!"

Her eyes were on his face. They had not yet looked elsewhere.

He put her on her feet, still holding her close to him.

"I think we shall die here."

She assented with a nod.

Her face was pale but that was all.

She seemed to read his heart with her eyes.

"You know I love you," he said.

She answered with her eyes, and drew closer to him.

A fearful sob shook him.

"And you do not fear death with me?"

"I pray for it."

The words were whispered, but the sweet voice was firm.

He bent over her.

The hungry flames were almost licking their feet. Shrieks of agony, wails of despair, the crashing of fallen timber, the mad roaring of the angry fire—all filled the air with a confusion of terrible sounds.

He bent over her.

She looked up.

Their lips met.

The roof under them swayed and rocked, the flames in mad glee advanced and retreated; the towering wall before them tottered, crumbled, crashed.

The roof slid slowly down into the beckoning flames.

The lovers looked at each other.

Their eyes were the mirrors of their hearts.

They were happy.

CHAPTER XIX.

BEYOND THE FIRE.

Down, down, sank the roof.

Grace was now in Clinton's close embrace.

The useless ladder lay by his side.

It was hard to give up the world so young, but they looked happy and contented.

Down, down sank their unstable platform.

When would the hot flames wrap them in its withering arms?

A sudden jar!

It had caught against some yet standing wall.

They were floating in a sea of fire.

Clinton looked up.

In sinking down the roof had also swept forward and had come nearer the roof of the wing, with which it was now almost on a level.

A flash of hope shot through Clinton's heart.

Would the ladder reach across?

It was a wild thought!

With the energetic man, to think and to act were one.

One quick, powerful toss of the ladder and both ends rested on firm supports.

Firm for how long?

Never mind—it was death, anyhow.

A fragile, precarious bridge over a yawning chasm of death!

Could he accomplish the journey in safety?

Clinton asked himself no such question.

Life and happiness—with Grace on his bosom he thought of nothing else—lay on the other side.

He was half way over, stepping swiftly, cautiously from round to round.

The roof behind began to sink again.

Quick, Clinton, quick!

They are safe.

Yes, safe upon the other roof, and comparatively out of danger.

"Grace, my own sweet love, life lies before us now. Can you say again, with your own dear lips this time, that you love me?"

But Grace was unconscious.

The next day there was a flight to the city in borrowed garments, in order that the burned wardrobes might be renewed.

Each day Clinton saw Grace for but a short time only, passing the remainder of the time in restless pacing of his room or midnight prowling of the streets.

He had told his love when death seemed at his elbow; and now that life was his, his soul was tortured by remorse.

When he was with her he forgot; when he left her fleet-footed memory overtook his conscience and anguish gnawed his heart.

An end there must be to this.

He would keep his appointment with Tete-de-Fer.

"Who knows," he caught at a floating straw of hope.

"He may not have the handkerchief. And then—and then——"

Well, what then?

Would that blot out the past? Would that make him a free man?

Perhaps not, but he would not plan until he knew.

He bade Grace good-by, saying he might be gone a day or a week, he could not tell, but he would write daily.

She kissed him, and he went.

CHAPTER XX.

THE INITIALS.

The impassive Monsieur Roche stood in the cell with Tete-de-Fer.

"Well?" was all he said.

"Here," replied the man joyously, drawing forth a package.

With steady hands Monsieur Roche opened the package, and took out a white silk handkerchief, almost new.

"It has not been used much," he said.

He avoided looking at the initials in one corner.

"No, my sister has kept it carefully, almost as if she knew its value."

"This is the handkerchief you stole from the man?"

"Found, if monsieur pleases," said Tete-de-Fer, with an attempt at pleasantry.

"I suppose," said Monsieur Roche, coldly, "a theft is a joke to a murderer."

Tete-de-Fer joked no more with his visitor.

Monsieur Roche turned the handkerchief in his hands, and looked at the initials.

What did he dread?

Did he fear he would learn too much from that silent witness?

Perhaps; but he looked.

"G. A.," he murmured.

And a sigh of relief broke from him.

Without thinking he knew the initials revealed nothing.

Had he not met Grace he would have cursed his luck that so much time and expense had come to so little.

Now he was glad.

Why?

It did not bring him nearer his happiness.

No, but it deferred the day when he must act.

The energy lent by hate had left him. It was love now that filled his soul, and it was rather despair than energy that urged him on.

He was glad to put the evil out of sight—behind him anyhow.

Let him enjoy his love yet awhile.

His heart cried out for peace.

The furious bursts of passionate anger which had overwhelmed him formerly at the thought of the wicked woman who had ruined his life, did not come any more.

The pure love of a true woman had triumphed, and since the night of the fire he hated no more.

He despaired.

"These initials tell me nothing."

"Perhaps not, monsieur; but they are a clew. Besides, I warned you that it was only as you see."

Tete-de-Fer was alarmed lest his visitor should repudiate his part of the contract.

"Have no fear. You shall be free, and you shall have the money."

"Fifteen thousand francs?"

"Yes."

"And when shall I be free?"

"To-day or to-morrow. Soon anyhow. Your conviction was a mistake. The man you robbed was a detective, the money was bad, you were only a tool."

"Then I have been tricked and played with."

Tete-de-Fer was furious, and made as if to rush at his visitor.

"Keep cool, *ami*. Remember I am Bras-de-Fer. Besides, you are not free yet, and if I wished to keep you, I have yet a few murders on hand that were real. I needed you, and I used you. If I need you again, I will use you again, and you shall never escape me."

Tete-de-Fer believed Monsieur Roche. He believed usually when that gentleman spoke in that tone.

Perhaps the iron arm was an argument, too. But whatever the cause, Tete-de-Fer had a profound respect for, and believed in, Monsieur Roche.

" How shall I be free, then?" he asked, humbly.

" Your lawyer will get out a writ of *habeas corpus* when he knows the facts, and that will be to-day. Then your case will be reviewed, and you will be free.

" And the money?"

" The day you are free go to Dan Hartley, the detective, and he will give it to you. I will pay your lawyer's charges.

" Thanks, monsieur; you will not forget?"

He meant to say " you will not play me false," but did not dare.

CHAPTER XXI.

THE INITIALS ONCE MORE.

Never had the Marquis d'Iberri been more gay and joyous than when he rejoined Grace, and with her and her aunt and her brother set out for the country.

A more quiet spot than the fashionable watering-place was selected, considerably to the disgust of Alphonse, who loved the crowd and all it meant.

He played the elder brother dutifully for a time—a week, perhaps—and then excusing himself to his sister and aunt, who seemed glad to be rid of him, he borrowed some more money of the marquis and left.

Clinton was not sorry to have him go, for he had no sympathy with the profligate pleasure which Alphonse most enjoyed, and yet for Grace's dear sake he would not treat her brother other than politely.

He had put every consideration likely to give him pain out of sight.

He had made up his mind that as matters were he could do no more.

He would not give himself up to an idle pursuit of a clew that led him nowhere.

Happy he would be now, without a single qualm. By

and by he could uncover his sorrow. Then would be time
enough to contemplate it and his future.

And it was easy to forget with Grace ever at his side.

She said little of her love, but he could read it in every
breath she drew, every beat of her heart.

Often he would look up and find her eyes fixed wistfully
on him as if studying his inmost nature.

"Well, little woman, what do you see on my heart?"

"GRACE, DARLING," HE SAID, ONE DAY, "I HAVE A
CONFESSION TO MAKE."

The wistful look would change into a bright glance of
answering love.

"Oh," she might reply, "it's written all over with 'I
love you!'"

"So it is, my Grace, and everything else is crowded
out."

"Grace darling," he said, one day, "I have a confession
to make."

The color died out of her cheeks, and a pleading look filled her eyes.

"Oh, it's nothing alarming," he laughed, "so don't look so frightened."

"Did I look frightened?"

"Indeed you did. You made me think of the description I've seen in story-books about a wounded doe at bay."

"I don't like confessions," she faltered; "they suggest such possibilities."

Clinton turned pale at this.

He thought of the possibilities of a confession he could make if he chose.

"Ah, well, little woman," he said, recovering himself, "this confession is full of pleasant possibilities."

"I'm foolish, dear," she said, brightly. "Come, make me this confession."

"Let me see. I must go back three years and a half. I was in Brest, in Upper Britanny. Were you ever there?"

"Yes," wonderingly. "Why, it was just about three years and a half ago!"

"Were you there then? How strange!"

Clinton affected great astonishment.

"Yes, and you knew it, too. Come, now, you naughty boy, confess in good earnest."

"Well, I will, then. When I was in Brest I saw a lady— a rather young lady—driving by. I only saw her face, but, Grace, I fell straightway in love with her; and, Grace, I never got over it."

"Why, Honore!"

Grace held his face in her two little hands, and looked lovingly into his eyes.

"Why, Honore!"

It was the name he had adopted.

"And you have really and truly loved me all this time?"

"Really and truly, I loved you the moment I saw your face. That is why I started so when I first saw you in New York."

"I remember that night. Shall I tell you why I remember it?"

"Please?"

"Because that was the time I fell in love with you; and I never got over it," she said, repeating his words in sweet mockery.

Clinton was radiant. He exclaimed:

"Then I was your first and only love, just as you were my first and only love?"

Involuntarily he winced as he spoke.

The words "only love" called up the passionate scene in the square chamber.

She did not notice his start.

She did not answer him.

She put her hands in his, and looked him long and lovingly in the eyes.

It was answer enough.

"What a pretty picture!"

It was Alphonse who spoke. He had just come up.

"By my word, marquis, if I were an artist I would make a picture like that. All the lovers would like it, and I, without liking it, should be famous."

It was a poor jest; but it pleased Alphonse, and he laughed at it.

Clinton thought it was coarse, and frowned.

"When she is my wife," he thought, and stopped.

He did not allow himself to think of that yet; but what he intended to think was, that when she was his wife the brother should be kept at a distance.

At present, however, he must treat him well, if not cordially.

The talk soon became general, and drifted to the delightful topic of Alphonse Gorinot and what he had been doing.

Delightful at least to Alphonse; and he talked in his light, careless way until he was tired—and they, too.

"How very warm," he remarked, finally.

Making some show of interest, Clinton answered.

"Yes."

And felt in his pocket for his handkerchief.

It was not there.

He looked around.

It was lying near Alphonse, who was fanning himself with his own.

Clinton wiped the perspiration from his face, and looked bored.

Grace sympathized with him, and proposed returning to the house. They did so.

When Clinton dressed for dinner he laid his handkerchief on the bureau. When he took it up again, he noticed that it was differently marked from his.

His had been marked in silk by Grace's dainty fingers.

Looking at it more closely to see what initials they were, he uttered a cry, and angrily threw it from him.

"I thought I had laid that away so that I should not see it again until I was ready."

The initials were G. A.

He walked up and down his room until he had in a measure overcome the feelings which the unfortunate initials had aroused, and then opened his trunk, took out a small tin box, and unlocked it.

"I intended to put that in here, and thought I had."

He opened the box.

There, carefully folded up, lay a handkerchief.

Clinton had evidently made a mistake.

"Is there a fate in it that will not let me forget?" he asked himself, sadly.

He took out the handkerchief, carelessly shook it out, and glanced mechanically at the initials.

"What!"

He looked at the other handkerchief.

"Heavens!"

He passed his hand across his forehead.

Looked again.

"How came I by two such?"

Again he examined them. There could be no mistake.

The initials were the same.

CHAPTER XXII.

WHAT "G. A." STOOD FOR.

"What could it mean? What did it mean?"

These two questions Clinton asked himself over and over, and still could find no answer.

The perspiration stood in beads on his forehead.

Was it a message from Heaven—a reminder of his duty?

Was it a trick to mislead him?

Was he known and watched?

Had he deceived himself in supposing that Clinton Hastings, the poor artist, could not be recognized in the wealthy Honore Beaumartin, the Marquis d'Iberri?

He looked in the mirror.

Clinton Hastings' face had been covered with a long brown beard.

The Marquis d'Iberri had a face as smooth as a child's. It was kept so by constant shaving.

Had the beard been a mask, it could not have disguised him more.

" No, he did not deceive himself; he was unrecognizable.

Up and down ·the room he paced, going over the same ground again and again, until the sound of the bell startled him from his unhappy dream.

He hurried down stairs to find Grace anxiously waiting for him on the veranda.

Usually it was he who waited for her.

His face showed the perturbation of his mind, and Grace noticed it.

All traces of his emotion died away ere he had fairly reached her side, but the unwonted expression troubled her.

" Is anything the matter, dear?"

" Nothing, darling—that is, nothing of any consequence, now that I have you by my side."

He looked fondly at her.

" Do you know, Grace dear," he said, a moment later, " that to me you are like one of the sirens in the fable; the sound of your voice so entrances me that I forget everything else but you. A little while ago I was very much troubled, but the moment you looked at me and said in that sweet voice of yours, 'Honore,' I forgot all my troubles."

" I am glad, dear, if I help you so. I hope it will always be the same."

" Oh, it will, my darling, it will. How can it be otherwise? It is not only your voice. A touch of your little hand, a glance of your loving eye, the rustle of your gown even, anything by you or of you, acts like magic with me.

" I think," he went on, with a loving smile, " that you must be my fate, I am so completely swallowed up in you. I think my soul lives in your body, and that you are my heaven."

" You do love me very much, do you not?"

The pleading tenderness in her voice, and the wistful questioning in her glance upward at him, made Clinton long to hold her in his arms and rain kisses on her sweet lips.

But there were too many spectators, and he had to content himself with a furtive pressure of her hand and the spoken assurance.

"My darling, I do not believe your own loving heart ever can comprehend what my heart feels. It is not only a love that would make me die for you. That would be nothing. It is a blind infatuation, an insane worship. You are my deity. Beyond you I cannot see. You are the end of my life."

"Oh, Honore!"

She seemed a little frightened.

"Was it too vehement, darling?

"I was fearful lest you should some day wake from your dream and find that I am only clay after all, and that maybe you would not love me so well then."

"Have no such fear, my Grace. If I am dreaming, be sure I shall never wake."

"You will always love me, won't you, Honore?"

She spoke almost beseechingly.

"Forever."

"And you would not let anything turn you from me?"

"Grace, my own darling!"

They were alone on the porch now, the other guests having gone to the dining-room.

"You are the purest, loveliest, most innocent creature that ever lived."

He took her hands in his and gazed with passionate earnestness into her upturned face.

"When I first saw you I did not know that, though I believed it from your angel face; but I loved you anyhow. If you were as bad as you are good, I should still love you. I could not help it."

A bright smile illumined her sweet face, and with a bewitching transition to gayety which set well upon her, Grace poised her head on one side, and pursing up her red lips, said:

"Seal the compact."

With her mood his mood changed, and in place of the

vehement earnestness of a moment before was his old time joyous mockery.

Not a thought was there in his mind of initials, or anything else unpleasant.

As usual he was the life of the party at dinner, and dealt out witticisms lavishly.

His spirits were unusually gay, as if taking a holiday from the burden which had just oppressed him.

"I say, D'Iberri!"

It was Alphonse calling after him as he went to his room for the night.

"Much obliged for your handkerchief. Haven't seen mine, have you?"

"No," answered Clinton, his thoughts wholly on Grace.

He took the handkerchief and went to his room.

He did not light his lamp, but sat by the open window, still dreaming of his love.

Little by little, however, freed now from the fascination of her presence, his thoughts reverted to the initials, and again he was a prey to the darkest forebodings.

Suddenly the words of Alphonse recurred to him.

A laugh of joy broke from him.

"There," said he to himself. "How I have worried over that, and here all at once comes an easy solution. For once, Alphonse, I could overcome my dislike for you, and fairly hug you. So, it was your handkerchief, then? Of course, of course."

He could have whistled, danced, shouted, in his glee at his discovery.

He remembered now that he had had his handkerchief out of his pocket, and it was evident that an unconscious exchange had been made.

He hastily lighted his lamp, and took out the box containing the two handkerchiefs.

"Dear me," he said. "How could I be so stupid?"

He took up the handkerchief belonging to Alphonse. He had tossed it unfolded into the box, and could make no mistake about it."

"'G. A.' indeed!"

He was very gleeful.

"Why, it's 'A. G.' just as plainly as can be. But that is like me. I go around chasing shadows so much that it's a wonder I don't have more scares. Alphonse, the next time you want to borrow five hundred I'll give you a thousand."

The little box was locked again with a snap, as if all of Clinton's cares were shut in there.

Indeed, Clinton, too, seemed to think so in good truth, for he fell asleep as peacefully as a tired child, and dreamed sweet dreams of his love.

And why not, since the dreadful "G. A." had melted into the harmless "A. G."

CHAPTER XXIII.

WHAT GRACE SAID ABOUT THE INITIALS.

Early morning saw Clinton up and dressed, humming merrily one of the Breton peasant ballads which he had picked up in his artist rambles in Britanny.

By and by the handkerchief caught his eye, and he smiled.

"How could I have made such a mistake?"

He picked it up and studied the initials.

"I don't know, though; they could pass for G. A. easily enough. I'll take a look at the other one."

Out came the little box.

Clinton shook his head and frowned as he compared the two handkerchiefs.

"There isn't a particle of difference. Now, that's stupid. There ought to be some way of telling which is the first and which the second letter. That's the worst of your monograms; you never can tell. There's mine, now."

He looked lovingly at the initials on his own handkerchief, and wished it was late enough to see Grace.

"I don't believe——"

He was very indifferent and philosophical about it now.

"I don't believe Alphonse himself could tell which was which. Funny how just alike they are. They might have been done by the same person; and yet one is G. A., and the other A. G."

A startled look shot into his eyes.

"Why! That's so! How do I know this other is G. A.? Why mightn't it be A. G., too?

"Gracious!"

"There now, Clinton, don't be a fool again. You worried about that enough last night. It's a strange coincidence, that's all."

The handkerchief was thrown petulantly into the box, and locked up.

" I won't look at that cursed thing again until——"

Well, what was the use of setting a time?

Clinton assumed his happy look again, and began to hum.

But his mind would keep running on those initials.

"A. G., G. A., I wonder which it is?"

The box was out again, and once more the initials were studied.

"Well," when he had scrutinized the letters with anxious care, "well, and suppose you do stand A. G.? What then? Is there anything in that?"

Clinton demanded this of the handkerchief in a defiant tone, as if to prove that it was a very small matter.

Again the box was closed and put away.

This time angrily.

" I'll not stay here, and be worried by this foolish trifle."

Thrusting Alphonse's handkerchief into his pocket, he went down stairs, and wandered uneasily about the porch until Grace came down, looking, as he told her, as fresh and rosy as Aurora.

He was speedily out of his own world and into hers, and was reveling in the joy of her presence.

All at once his hand came in contact with the handkerchief, and a bright idea occurred to him.

" Grace, I did have Alphonse's handkerchief, after all."

" Yes?"

" Yes; and, very stupidly, 1 never thought it was his when he spoke about it."

" No?"

Grace was not vitally interested in the handkerchief, but she was quite willing to hear her lover talk about anything.

"No. I had found it in my pocket, and thought the initials were G. A. Now wasn't 1 stupid?"

" Of course you weren't stupid, you couldn't be."

" Well, but see if you could have made G. A. out of it."

He gave her the handkerchief.

" In a hurry I might. Of course I could, easily."

" Now, Grace, you are trying to evade the question, and that isn't like my honest little woman."

" Why, Honore, you are in earnest."

Grace spoke feelingly.

Clinton all at once recognized that he was making a serious matter of this trifle again.

He was angry with himself.

" Dear little Grace, what a fool I am!"

" I'll never agree to any such thing, Honore."

Grace smiled. Clinton smiled and bent over her.

" Somebody will catch you doing that some day," said Grace, a moment later.

"Now's a good opportunity then."

And Clinton repeated his former action.

The handkerchief was now far away from his thoughts, but Grace had not forgotten it, for she held it in her hand.

" Don't you see," she said, " the A. is on the top of the G., and that shows how it is intended to be read?"

" There, my love," he exclaimed, gayly, "you denied that I was stupid, and then you go to work and prove that I am."

" You are not stupid; only you're a man——"

" Oh, I see; you think that all men are naturally stupid."

" Honore, you shall not kiss me again for two hours if you interrupt me to say such things. I was going to say that men are not expected to know much about such matters."

Of course Clinton could not be alone with Grace every minute of the day.

There were whole hours at times when he was left to his own devices. These periods he usually spent lolling on the porch, waiting for Grace and dreaming about her.

To-day he found that his thoughts would continually revert to the initials, until at last he petulantly went to his room determined to have it out with those irritating letters.

Once more he took out the box and examined the initials. He was going to try them by Grace's test. Then he would at least know what the initials really were, and perhaps he could then get them out of his mind.

By the test they were A. G.

"There! That is settled. A. G. you are then. Now I hope I shall have some peace.

"Well, and what if A. G. does stand for Alphonse Gorinot? Bah, Clinton, you drivel like an idiot."

But the idea was not thus to be driven from his mind. It stuck there and haunted him like a nightmare.

Not that he connected Alphonse with the masked man, that thought had not yet suggested itself; but as if he were bewitched by them they kept going through his mind, a sort of refrain to every other thought.

"A. G., Alphonse Gorinot. A. G., Alphonse Gorinot."

"You must be sick, Clinton," he said to himself. "You have not been taking the exercise you should. Tear yourself away from Grace for an afternoon and go for a long walk. You'll be sick if you don't."

And he went that very afternoon, explaining to Grace that he felt the need of hard, exercise which he was accustomed to.

Grace urged him to go, for she saw that he did not look like himself.

CHAPTER XXIV.

A. G.—ALPHONSE GORINOT.

A. G.—Alphonse Gorinot. A. G.—Alphonse Gorinot.

Despite his most strenuous efforts to think of other things this refrain kept dancing through his brain.

It kept tune to his steps as he walked along.

A. G.—Alphonse Gorinot. A. G.—Alphonse Gorinot, until he was nearly beside himself.

Could it be a symptom of brain fever? Might it be a possible indication of insanity?

He quickened his pace, and still every footfall was only a time beat to

A. G.—Alphonse Gorinot. A. G.—Alphonse Gorinot.

He ran, and the farmers working in their fields marveled to see him going at that mad pace in the broiling sun.

The refrain only quickened its time to keep up with him.

Weary at last, and angry with himself, he stopped by the edge of a wood and sat down.

"Now I will face this thing. I have tried to run away from it, and it has clung to me. I will meet it and kill it with reasoning.

" Why should I dislike to look the matter squarely in the face?"

He did not know. Indeed, he was not conscious that underneath his unwillingness was an undefined dread. But there was.

"A. G.—Alphonse Gorinot. Well, and may not A. G. stand for a thousand other persons?

"This A. G. could not stand for Alphonse Gorinot; now be reasonable, and see how absurd such a thought would be."

Clinton was addressing his mind as if it belonged to somebody else. It was a habit he had fallen into in his lonely artist days.

"Well, if you will have it, say it does stand for Alphonse. Will you have the folly to suppose that Alphonse and the masked man——

"Clinton, Clinton would you dishonor yourself by allowing such a thought one moment's rest in your mind? Can you forget that he is Grace's brother?

"Out upon you, fiend, that would suggest such a thought. Out—out, I will not listen! I will not! I will not!"

Once more he was striding furiously along the road, his hands clenched, his jaws set, and his lips convulsively muttering:

"I will not! I will not!"

And yet he did.

Again he stopped and sat under a tree.

"I will then. Forgive me, Grace, darling. It is not I. It is the fiend that possesses me.

"Well, then, Satan, have your say. Insinuate what you will. But have a care; I will not be driven too far."

Clinton spoke as if he really believed Satan had possession of his mind.

"Alphonse is the same height, you say? Well, and might not fifty thousand men be the same?

"Something in his voice and manner that wakens memory? Bah, you are fanciful. Why did you not think of that before?

"I did?

"I did not. It's a lie. I thought I had seen him before. I knew afterward that it was only an undefined resemblance to Grace.

"Aha! Are you satisfied now?

"What! The woman like Grace?

"Now, stop! Stop! Another thought like that and I will tear your heart out with my own fingers.

"My Grace! My pure-hearted, innocent Grace! Oh! great Heaven, am I going mad?"

He held his head in his hands, and his eyes glared fearfully. It seemed as if his brain were on fire—as if it were no longer under his control.

"I cannot bear this!" he cried, in agony. "I cannot, and I will not. Oh! Heaven have mercy!"

He threw himself on the ground, and held his face in his hands. He believed he was really going mad.

Still the refrain went on, with a frightful addition now.

A. G.—Alphonse Gorinot. Grace was the woman.

A. G.—Alphonse Gorinot. Grace was the woman.

A frightful calm came over Clinton.

"I will tear you out of my brain. With red hot pincers I will tear you out. I will not go mad. Not yet anyhow. I will tell Grace all. I should have done so before. This is my punishment, and I deserve it. I that would have deceived that gentle creature! I that have polluted her pure lips by mine that have been pressed lovingly against those others.

"What will Grace do? What? Heaven help me, whatever she does!

"Send me from her in scorn and loathing? It would be right, and then I should turn devil again and accomplish my infernal mission.

"Turn from me in pity, and die alone, away from me, of a broken heart! That is more like my Grace.

"My Grace! Oh, Heaven, what mockery! My Grace! and I her murderer!

"But it must be done—it must be done!"

Slowly, sadly, sternly, Clinton rose and wended his way homeward.

No longer was he tormented by the maddening refrain. It was as if his resolve had exorcised the demon in his brain.

But, oh! the pain that racked his heart at the thought of what Grace would feel, how she would look, when he told her of his unhappy past!

It was only right. He could see it plainly now, though he had so successfully put it out of sight before.

But how could he live without her love?

Alas! that was not the question.

Before him, he saw two ways—one right, full of anguish; one wrong, full of madness.

There could be no choice.

If Grace were one whit less an angel, he might have felt that he could withhold from her the truth.

Yes, he must tell it to her—he must.

But need he tell it now, right away? Might he not wait a little while?

He caught eagerly at the hope of a respite.

Why wait? Would it not be putting off the evil day, merely? Could any relief come by waiting?

No, there was no use waiting in hope of anything occurring to help him, and yet the nearer he approached the house the greater his disinclination became to tell Grace his story.

He stopped within sight of the house and discussed the matter with himself.

No good reason could he give himself for delaying the confession, and only one excuse could he find for waiting.

That excuse he rejected twenty times.

At first angrily, and finally doubtfully.

"What would be the use of trying such a desperate plan? I know it could only result in giving pain to an innocent man."

Then he turned to the thought of telling Grace. That was unbearable.

"But since he is innocent, it could only be a joke to him, and at least it would drive out of my head this infernal refrain, which I know will come back if I give up my intention to confess the whole truth to Grace.

"I will do it. He may be gone, but I don't believe it."

CHAPTER XXV.

TETE-DE-FER MEETS AN OLD ACQUAINTANCE.

In that same little French tavern on Mott street where once before we have been, sat very nearly the same disreputable crew of Frenchmen, playing *vingt-et-un*.

It seemed as if the game might be the very same one. The oaths, the exclamations of chagrin or pleasure, the shuffling of the cards, seemed the same done over again.

And no wonder. The same men played the same game day after day and month after month, except when a more unfortunate rascal than his fellows was caught by the law and retired from society for a time.

Even then the vacant place was filled and the game went on with a laugh for the comrade who was taking his enforced vacation.

So they sat one warm, summer afternoon.

"Ah, good-day, *mes amis*. At it still, eh?"

"Bras-de-Fer! Bras-de-Fer!"

The welcoming shout rose, and every man turned in his chair to hail the masterful fellow who lost his money so cheerfully.

One man only sat still and said nothing.

It was Tete-de-Fer, who was wondering what had happened to bring the detective there.

Bras-de-Fer caught his eye.

"Aha, my iron-headed comrade, you are here, then! They told me you had been studying the banking system too hard, and were sick abed in consequence."

A quickly hushed laugh followed this reference to Tete-de-Fer's capture and imprisonment.

The crowd dared to laugh when Bras-de-Fer joked, but they stopped when Tete-de-Fer glanced angrily around the table.

"Yes, I am here; and I may as well tell you I do not like such jokes."

The men about the room looked at each other. Tete-de-Fer was more dreaded, though less feared, than Bras-de-Fer. The two had always been friendly. Were they going to have a row now? They waited for the strong man's answer.

"It was a joke then, eh? I'm glad to know that, for I was afraid, when I looked at your head, that you really had had a bad fever."

Tete-de-Fer's head still showed the marks of the prison barber.

Nobody laughed this time, excepting Bras-de-Fer, who seemed to enjoy his jest very much. Everybody looked to see Tete-de-Fer jump at his tormentor with his knife. They knew his violent temper.

They were disappointed. Tete-de-Fer scowled sullenly, but neither moved nor spoke.

Bras-de-Fer laughed carelessly, and called for wine. The glasses were filled.

" We'll drink to the better health of our friend Tete-de-Fer."

The men looked sidewise at each other. They hesitated to offend Tete-de-Fer.

" You will drink, my friends," said Bras-de-Fer, imperiously.

They drank. They would have crawled on the floor if the order had been given in that tone.

Tete-de-Fer's glass was untouched.

" My friend"—Bras-de-Fer looked directly at him—"you will not offend me by not drinking?"

The glass was slowly, sullenly raised and drained.

" Good! I thought you would drink if I asked you in the right way."

Tete-de-Fer muttered a curse under his breath.

It was dangerous trifling with such a wild beast, but Clinton was in a mood when he was glad of any such rough pastime.

He disliked to use the man for the purpose he intended, and it was a relief to him in his reckless frame of mind to take the chances of rousing a rebellious spirit.

" Come, friend banker," he said; "let you and I take a walk together and discuss the new system."

Tete-de-Fer got up and followed, much to the wonderment of the crowd.

" Bras-de-Fer is the devil !" said one, when the two were gone.

" And see how the fierce Tete-de-Fer followed him like a whipped puppy!" said another.

The two men sat together in Bras-de-Fer's room.

" Why did you gibe me so?" growled Tete-de-Fer.

" To show you, and everybody else, that I am master."

If Tete-de-Fer expected to be conciliated, he was mistaken.

" I thought you were through with me?"

" As long as you live, I shall use you as often as I wish."

" If I should refuse?"

"When you do I will tell you. Do you refuse now?"

"Tell me what you want."

"Do you refuse?"

"No."

"That is more like it. Now, I'll tell you what I want. Would you like to make a thousand dollars?"

"Of course."

"Well, if I were to find the masked man of Chateau d'Iberri for you, do you think you could make a thousand dollars?"

"Have you found him? You must be the devil!"

"Only half-brother, *mon ami*. Yes, I have found the masked man. You will go to him, and tell him who you are, and as much of the affair as you think necessary, excepting that you must not mention Chateau d'Iberri."

"Where is he?"

"I will take you to him. If he should insist that he is not the man, pretend to believe him, and come away. If he gives in, ask him for a thousand dollars at once. If he should not give in, I will see that you get the money."

"What is his name?"

"You need not know that. I will point him out. As soon as you have the money, or he has refused to give it, come back here at once, and wait for me, if you have to wait a week."

"I will. You order like an emperor, though."

"Don't I pay like one, too?"

"Yes."

CHAPTER XXVI.

A LOAN OF ONE THOUSAND DOLLARS.

"I am so glad to see you again, Honore!"

"And I you, Grace, dear. The two days seemed like two years. But I shall have to leave you again to-morrow."

"Oh! But you look better than you did, Honore. Why, you looked dreadfully troubled for a day or two, though you tried to hide it from me that you were so. By and by, you will tell me when anything troubles you, won't you, dear?"

"Indeed I will. I would tell you now, only I don't——"

"I say, D'Iberri. Excuse me, Grace, I want to have a word with D'Iberri in private."

Clinton turned pale as he followed Alphonse away. But, pshaw! why should he feel uncomfortable?

"You'll think I'm a regular shark, D'Iberri, but the truth is, I'm awfully pushed. One of my creditors in the city insists on having a payment. Got any cash to spare?"

Clinton would have given ten thousand dollars with joy if he could have been sure Alphonse was speaking only the truth.

"How much?"

"Well, I don't think less than a thousand would be of any use."

"A thousand! I'll tell you what, Alphonse, I've got to go to the city to-morrow, so if you'll give me the bill, I'll draw my check for it, and pay it in full. I know what a nuisance these duns are."

Alphonse looked as if he did not like the suggestion.

"Good of you, D'Iberri; but, to be frank, the man is in the village, and says he wants the cash."

"Oh, nonsense! Bring him up here, and let him take my check."

"D'Iberri, I'll let you into a secret. I've fooled this chap so often that he's suspicious, and swears he'll expose my troubles by a suit if I don't pay cash right away."

"But he's unreasonable, Alphonse; he surely can't suppose you carry so much cash at once. Come, let's go see him, and I'll get him to take my check. I don't believe I have cash enough."

"No, I won't let you have any such trouble, D'Iberri. See if you have the cash. If not, I'll tell him he must wait, that's all."

Alphonse looked very determined, and so little worried, that, in spite of the most direful misgivings, Clinton, who was anxious to believe him, told himself that the demand for money at this time was only a coincidence.

He knew he had the money, because he had drawn that much to give to Tete-de-Fer.

He gave the thousand dollars to Alphonse, and returned as quickly as possible to Grace, feeling that he needed the forgetfulness of her companionship more than ever.

"Honore," said Grace, when he had joined her, "you

look annoyed. It is Alphonse, I know. He has been borrowing money of you. I have known for some time that he
was making use of you in this way; but, though I was indignant, I said nothing. Now I will not have it any
more."

"Why, Grace, dear, I don't care for the money. I'm so
rich that I'm glad of some one to help me spend my money.
But, to be candid, I don't like to think of your brother
being such a fellow as Alphonse."

"I don't, either, darling, and I will not have him
troubling you so. Was it on his account that you looked
so troubled before?"

"No, no; that is, not exactly, Grace. But don't talk of
him. Let us talk of you."

*   *   *   *   *

"Well, my iron-headed friend, did you collect your
thousand dollars?"

"I did."

Clinton shuddered. He had hoped to hear otherwise.

"Did you have any trouble?"

"Not much. He swore at first it was a mistake; but, as
soon as I'd talked a little with him, I knew him dead certain, and I let him see he couldn't play with me."

"How did he pay you?"

"Bills. Here they are."

Clinton looked them over. They were the same he had
given Alphonse.

"Did you make any agreement with him?"

"No; he wanted me to leave the country, but I said no.
You see I didn't know what you wanted."

"That was right. You may go now. Come back here
to-morrow morning, and I'll show you how to make another thousand. You haven't any doubt he was the masked
man?"

"I can swear to him; besides, would he have paid if he
hadn't been?"

"All right. Come in the morning."

When Tete-de-Fer was gone, Clinton mechanically
locked the door after him, and threw himself on a chair,
murmuring:

"Just Heaven! what does this mean? Whither does it

lead me? Poor Grace, when you know that your brother—ah!"

He sprang wildly to his feet.

"Oh, Heaven! not that—not that! Keep me from such thoughts. Back me with pain, cut my heart in shreds, tear my soul from my body, but, oh, Heaven, spare me such thoughts.

"Make me crazy if you will, trample me in the dust, do what you will, but not that—not that.

"It could not be that. You know it could not be that."

He was pleading like a little child now, and it seemed as if his mind was unsettled.

"How could it be so? She is so good, so pure, so gentle, so innocent.

"Not that, please—not that. I will go away and hide myself. I will die!"

He fell on his knees, and wept, and prayed, and pleaded.

Then of a sudden his mood changed, and he clutched and tore at his throat, blaspheming and cursing.

He shattered the furniture into pieces, fell upon the bed, and rent it in his insane fury.

Again he pleaded and prayed upon his knees.

Again he raved and blasphemed.

He fell upon the floor shrieking with wild laughter.

CHAPTER XXVII.

WHAT THE NEIGHBORS THOUGHT.

Rap—rap—rap!

"Come in."

An ineffectual attempt to open the door.

"I can't open it."

"Oh! I'll unlock it. Come in."

"*Gloire de Ciel!*"

Tete-de-Fer looked wonderingly around the room, and then at Bras-de-Fer.

"Pandemonium broke loose," said Bras-de-Fer, with a loud laugh.

"That's what your neighbors said to me as I came up. Too much——"

Tete-de-Fer filled out his sentence by a motion suggestive of emptying a glass down his throat.

"That's it. I only do it once in a while, but when I do, I make a business of it."

"It looks like it."

The room was a perfect wreck. Not a piece of furniture was whole.

Rap—rap—rap!

"Come in."

A frightened face peered into the room, and with distended eyes viewed the scene.

"Was monsieur ill?"

"Hand me that pillow, Tete-de-Fer. Ill, did you ask, *mon ami?* Come in, please."

But the owner of the face had his eye on the pillow, and begged to be excused.

"Then get out."

With a shout of laughter, Bras-de-Fer launched the pillow at the door with such good aim that if the face had not been suddenly withdrawn there is a likelihood that it would have been squeezed somewhat.

This was a new mood for Tete-de-Fer to find the detective in, and he hardly knew how to conduct himself lest he should become a victim.

"Are you ready to see me?" he ventured to say.

"Ready? Of course I'm ready. Don't I look so?"

"I didn't know but you might be tired from last night's exertions."

"Tired! oh, no. I feel like doing more. I'd like to get hold of a good stout man and tear him to pieces."

Tete-de-Fer laughed uneasily.

"What do you want me to do?"

"You are sure you are willing to do it?"

"Oh! quite sure."

"I wish you'd refuse."

"Why?"

"Because I could try my hand on you then."

"Thank you, monsieur; I'd rather you'd try somebody else."

Tete-de-Fer tried to appear at ease but failed utterly. His discomfiture seemed to give Clinton great pleasure. He had at last thoroughly tamed this wild beast.

"I'll tell you what I want you to do. You're to go to that chap again. You know?"

"Yes."

"Tell him you'll leave the country if he will give you another thousand dollars. Tell him you want to go to Australia. If he says he can't get the money tell him jewels will do. Make him give the money or its value. Do you hear?"

"Yes."

"You want to watch your time to-morrow so as to catch him just about dusk—a little before it will be best. You understand?"

"Yes."

"That will make it dark when he returns to you, so take care he doesn't stick a knife in your ribs."

"I'll take care."

Tete-de-Fer shook a heavy stick in his hand in a significant manner.

"None of that, *ami*. I don't want him hurt. I'm saving him for better things."

"All right; but suppose he tries?"

"Just give his wrist a tap—you know the trick, and then take his knife and bring it here. I want it to put with my curiosities."

"All right."

"Now don't forget. Just before dusk."

CHAPTER XXVIII.

HOW ALPHONSE GOT A THOUSAND MORE.

It was dusk.

Clinton and Grace sat lovingly together at one end of the porch.

All the other guests had gone to have a moonlight view of the famous waterfall some distance away.

The lovers thought they were to have a quiet evening alone, when to their annoyance they could distinguish the figure of a man coming up the walk.

"D'Iberri, where are you?"

It was Alphonse.

"Here I am."

"Ah! they told me I should find you hereabouts. I'd like to see you for a moment."

"Certainly. Excuse me, darling."

"Honore, refuse to give him any more money. I know that is what he is after."

Grace whispered this to her lover.

"I shall have to to-night, dear, for I am run short myself."

And Clinton joined Alphonse.

"I say, D'Iberri, how are you for cash? The ugliest of my creditors is after me, and threatens all sorts of things if I don't pay at once."

"I am very sorry, Alphonse, but I haven't ten dollars with me."

"*Mon Dieu!* What shall I do? Let me see. I'll tell you. Can't you draw a check to bearer. That's the same as cash almost."

"Yes, or I could draw it just as well to your order or the creditor's. What's his name?"

"If you don't mind, old fellow, I'll not tell you. It's not nice to have one's creditors known, don't you see?"

"Of course. Then I'll draw it to your order, eh?"

"Better make it bearer, I guess."

"All right. You are sure a thousand will do? I can let you have more just as well."

"That's awfully good of you, D'Iberri. You're the most generous fellow I ever saw. Suppose you let me have another check for five hundred."

"Oh, pshaw! Say a thousand. I'll never miss it."

"A thousand, then. How can I thank you?"

"Don't try. Come up to my room."

Alphonse followed with a springy step, and a low, joyous whistle. D'Iberri was as good as a bank.

Clinton opened his trunk, took out his check-book, and drew two checks as agreed.

"Now isn't it odd," exclaimed Alphonse, with a sort of innocent philosophy, "that your name should be worth so much more than mine? I could write my name to one of those sheets, and I couldn't get a cent for it. But you! I suppose now you could make that ten times as large and still the name would carry it."

Clinton smiled.

"One hundred or one thousand times as much I could carry with my name in Paris, but here it depends upon my deposit at the bank. You see I never have more than ten or twenty thousand here at one time, and sometimes it runs very close to nothing. I shouldn't wonder if this reduced me very low. I know I can't have much left. I'll count up, just for fun."

For an impecunious spendthrift like Alphonse this talk of money was a very agreeable one.

He followed Clinton's figures with great interest. What did he care if his creditors had to wait.

"What's this?" exclaimed Clinton, in a tone of perplexity.

"What's what?"

"Why, it looks as if I'd used up my balance completely."

"Pshaw! Well, then, old fellow, just cut me down half on that thousand for myself."

Alphonse could afford to be generous.

"Yes, but the balance is gone without counting the two thousand to you."

"*Mon Dieu!*"

Alphonse was very rudely startled out of his easy tranquillity.

"How could I have been so careless. I don't care for myself, Alphonse. It is only on your account."

"But surely the bank will let you overdraw."

"Indeed they will not. They have told me so very politely, but very firmly."

"Isn't there any way, then, you can let me have the money?"

"Not a way. Unless you can wait a few days, till I telegraph for more."

"I can't do that. *Mon Dieu!* what shall I do?"

"Is this creditor so very savage?"

"Awful."

"Try to put him off. Tell him who I am; let me see him, and perhaps he will listen to me."

"You couldn't do anything with him, D'Iberri. I'll have to try Grace. Maybe she will have it. I must get it somehow."

"Well, look here, Alphonse—I feel as if I was somehow to blame in this matter myself. I ought to have had the money on hand. If Grace shouldn't have the money, let me go with you and talk to this absurd fellow, will you?"

"I'll see Grace first."

"Well, you know I'm awfully sorry, now, don't you, Alphonse? I'll do a great deal for you for your own sake, but I'll do absolutely anything because you are Grace's brother."

Alphonse inwardly cursed him for a love-sick fool.

They returned to the porch, Clinton still profuse in his expressions of sympathy, Alphonse in a very bad humor.

And indeed it was enough to make any man lose his temper to be made to believe that he was not only to get rid of an importunate creditor, but was also to have an unexpected

"GRACE, MAY I SEE YOU A MOMENT, PLEASE?" WAS
HIS NOT VERY COURTEOUS REQUEST.

thousand presented to him, and then to have it all suddenly withdrawn without a word of warning.

"Grace, may I see you a moment, please?" was his not very courteous request.

As Grace had half expected such a summons, she made no answer, but went to him, leaving Clinton to sit down and wait for her.

"What do you want, Alphonse?"

"Come to your room and I will tell you."

"Why not here?"

"I can't very well."

"Now, Alphonse, if it is money you want, I can tell you now that I have none."

"If you knew what I had to say, you wouldn't stand here talking. Will you come?"

Wondering what he could mean, Grace called out:

"I'll be back in a few moments, Honore," and then followed Alphonse to her room.

Scarcely had she passed through the door than Clinton sprang from his chair, and, with marvelous agility, climbed up one of the porch supports, and crept along the roof, until he was under Grace's window.

The moon was not yet up, and the darkness was sufficient to conceal him from all but very prying eyes.

He heard the room door open and shut, and he could feel that each was waiting for the other to speak.

"Well," said Grace, at last, "what do you want with me?"

"I want one thousand dollars."

"You demand it like a highwayman, as if I must give it to you."

"And you must, for I need it badly."

"I have no such sum, as you must know."

"You have its equivalent."

"How?"

"Diamonds and other jewels."

"Why, Alphonse Gorinot!"

"Why, Madame Clinton Hastings!"

"Ah!"

It was a quick gasp.

"Well, then, give me the jewels."

"Are you robbing me? Has it come to this? Oh, Alphonse!"

"Come, Grace, that won't do. You ought to know that when I call you Madame Hastings I mean something."

"You mean to force me to do your will; but you ought to know that I am not without determination, too."

"Bah! If you will have the truth, which I was willing to keep from you, know that a man who witnessed the marriage has found me out, and demands a thousand dollars, or jewels equal in value to that amount."

"Why not refuse?"

"And have him tell the whole story? I fancy Marquis d'Iberri would be in a great hurry to marry Madame Hastings."

"He would believe anything I told him. He loves me."

"You're a fool, Grace. Suppose this man were to tell of the marriage?"

"I would confess it and say my husband was dead."

"A fine plan that would be. To say nothing of the disgrace of the secret and concealed marriage. You could not even prove that Hastings was dead."

"But, *mon Dieu,* you told me he was dead. Alphonse Gorinot, if you have deceived me!"

Grace's sweet voice was full of threatening.

"I haven't deceived you at all. He's dead enough. The man who is here is the one who killed him."

There were a few moments of silence. Then Grace spoke.

"If I give these jewels are you sure he will leave us in peace?"

"I have his promise."

"How much is that worth?"

"I don't know, but I do know that if he is kept waiting much longer he will probably come here to find me."

"Take the jewels. Help yourself. But, Alphonse, can you do nothing to rid us of this man for the future."

The voice was low, sweet, and pleading, but Clinton in his concealment shuddered at the fearful warning that was behind the words.

Alphonse laughed.

"I'll try, Grace. Now don't let young moneybags down stairs see that you are disturbed. Perhaps you'd better stay here, and I'll say you are sick."

"No, I'll go down."

"As you please. I'll go to my room and fix up the jewels. Good-by. Sorry to have troubled you."

When Grace returned to the porch Clinton was waiting for her, and it seemed to the fair young creature that he was never more tender and loving.

CHAPTER XXIX.

CLINTON ADDS TO HIS COLLECTION.

" You don't look well this morning, *mon ami.*

It was Bras-de-Fer's salutation to Tete-de-Fer.

" I might have looked worse."

" How so?"

Tete-de-Fer opened his shirt and showed a wound in his breast near the neck.

" Aha! He tickled you, did he?"

" Yes."

" And you. Did you not return the compliment?"

"He was too quick. Like a cat."

" This is good—very good."

Bras-de-Fer rubbed his hands, and looked pleased.

" I am glad you like it. I don't."

" Is that so? I am sorry for that, for it pleases me."

" Why?"

" You will hate him now."

" You want me hate him?"

" Very much."

" Why not let me tickle him then?"

" Oh, there is no hurry about that. I have use for him yet. When I am through I will turn him over to you. Did you get the knife?"

" Yes; here it is."

" A pretty little thing, eh? Why did you let him do it, when I warned you?"

" He was so quick."

" Bah! I wonder if he thinks he finished you?"

" I don't know. When he gave me the jewels I put them in my pocket, and then he jumped at me and gave me this. It was a good aim. A little higher and I would have been done for. I fell back and the knife slipped out of his hand. He'd have come for the jewels, I guess, but some people came along and he skipped. I got up and found I was only wounded, not seriously hurt."

"Good. I'll have it in the papers that you are dead, so don't let him see you again. Where are the jewels?"

"Here."

"They're worth a thousand. I'll give you two. Now you may leave America as soon as you please."

"You mean you want me to go?"

"Exactly."

"Where shall I go?"

"How would South America do?"

"Good. I'll go there."

"Tete-de-Fer?"

"Yes."

"You'll need more practice than you have yet to fool me."

"What do you mean?"

"I mean you lie! You are not going to South America with all that money of yours. You're going to Paris, so your sister can help you spend your fortune."

Tete-de-Fer looked confused.

"*Mon Dieu!*" continued Bras-de-Fer, in a tone of mockery. "What a tender affection between brother and sister! It quite makes me weep."

Tete-de-Fer looked up from under his eyebrows.

"Tell that dear Elise, when you see her, that her sisterly affection made Bras-de-Fer weep."

"You know her?"

"I know everybody, Robert Caradoc. I know the pretty Elise Candolet, of course. But there, don't be jealous of your sister, for she never knew me. Only don't lie to me. Now good-by, and unless you are hung in the meantime, I shall have some use for you before very long."

"How can you find me?"

Bras-de-Fer laughed sardonically.

"Leave me alone for finding pretty women, or ugly men. The pretty Elise or the ugly Robert. Be perfectly tranquil, *mon ami*. And now, quick, out of America, for by to-morrow morning the papers will have you dead, and little pig-sticker will be chuckling over his good aim. Some day, good Robert. Some day, eh? You will laugh then, eh?"

Tete-de-Fer ground his teeth. He liked neither the pleasantry of his master nor the thought of waiting for his revenge; but he did not even dare to think of disobeying.

Left alone, Clinton's face dropped its jovial expression and fell into the old stern lines.

"More trophies! Well, at least my task is easy now. I have them all in my grasp, every one. And one by one I will tighten the pressure on them until they all shall cry for mercy.

"Grace, too. The gentle, loving, innocent Grace!"

His mocking laughter was more fearful than his wildest denunciations had ever been.

"How she has held the chords of my heart in her hand! And the tender, seductive tune she has played on them!

"The blood-thirsty tigress! She sends a man to his death with a purr of divinest love. Inhuman wretch, how I will punish you! How I will gloat over your sufferings! Every heart-pang of mine shall vibrate tenfold to your anguish.

"How I hate you!

"How I love you!

"How I loathe you, scorn you, despise you!

"How I cling to you, worship you.

"I never loved you more than now. It is my punishment, perhaps.

"I long to sit by your side and drink in the honey of your words! to revel in the soft, seductive glance of your heavenly blue eyes.

"I am eager to put you on the rack of fear, to tear your soul with agony, to haunt you with specters of your past.

"As I would have spent my life in proving my love, had you been the angel you seem, so I will now spend my life in inventing tortures for your cruel heart.

"Ah, I can reach it, incredible as may be its wickedness and harshness. I will so study you that your waking hours shall be one long dream of horrors and your sleeping moments ages of anguish.

"Your slave I am, for I love you still. Your executioner I will be, for I hate you."

CHAPTER XXX.

FIXING A DAY.

When the morning papers from the city reached the little country town, Clinton noticed the eagerness with which Alphonse seized one and scanned its columns.

Passing behind Alphonse when he saw that his attention was fixed, he noted accurately which portion so held his eye, and waited until he could obtain the same paper.

When he did so and turned to the place he had mentally noted, he smiled grimly.

He read this paragraph, telegraphed from a small city not far from where they were spending the summer:

"UNACCOUNTABLE SUICIDE.—The body of an unknown man, evidently a foreigner, was found late last night about two miles from the city, on the turnpike road. It was still warm when found. A small dagger was tightly grasped in his hand, and a gaping wound in the chest, just over the heart, showed how he had come by his death. Suicide is suspected, as valuable jewels were found on his person. There is no clew to the motive. The body is lying in the morgue waiting identification."

An accurate description of Tete-de-Fer followed this paragraph.

Alphonse was very happy during the remainder of the day; and graciously accepted the check for a thousand dollars which Clinton offered him.

During the early part of the day Grace seemed nervous, but a brief conversation with her light-hearted brother had a soothing effect, and she was thereafter her own sweet, loving self.

It seemed to her that the marquis was almost fierce in his adoration of her, and she smiled tenderly when the avowals of his love were unusually vehement.

They were sitting together in a favorite spot under an apple tree on the brow of a hill. They were there safe from intrusion or concealed observation.

He was gazing at her with his whole soul in his eyes.

"Grace," he exclaimed, suddenly, "Why do I love you so passionately?"

She smiled bewitchingly.

"I don't know, Honore. Not on account of my deserts, I am sure."

"Oh, my darling! You deserve a greater, better love than mine. You are so pure, so innocent, so honest, so loving. Grace, darling, I know that if every act of your life were spread out here before me, I could find not one which would not glorify your saintly life.

"Don't contradict me. I know what you would say. You would tell me of faults. Heaven bless you! such faults as you could tell of would only intensify the whiteness of your soul.

"But it is not for your goodness that I love you. I loved you just as madly before I knew you.

"Ah!" he went on with exquisite fondness in his voice. I do believe you have cast magic spells about me.

"But I am glad your life has been so pure and innocent, darling. I am glad that I am your first and only love. I think that if you had been the ordinary sort of woman, ready to love any respectable man, free, perhaps, with caresses, I—but this is nonsense, isn't it, dear?"

"Nothing you say is nonsense."

She spoke faintly.

"You cannot wonder, can you, though, Grace, dear, if I rejoice in your freedom from guile? I am happy that I can say that my lips have never pressed any other woman's but yours, in love, and I am happy that yours have pressed only mine. Why, Grace!" he started, excitedly, "the very thought that you had ever spoken words of love to any other man would drive me distracted; and, if it were possible for me to believe that you had lavished such kisses as you have given me, on any other man, I would—would—why, Grace, I would—— *Mon Dieu!* my darling, I am glad you cannot see the demon which my idle thoughts have stirred up in my heart."

"Why think of such things, Honore?"

Grace looked pale and frightened.

"There, sweet one, forgive me. I think I am not sane about my love for you. I think if I were certain that I was worthy of you, I could be more serene. But when I am in your angel presence I feel most my unworthiness, and then

I think, suppose some better man should come along, and my Grace should—— But, ah! you would not, would you, Grace? If I thought the man lived who could win your love, or ever had, I would—I would—— Grace, the thought puts murder in my heart. There, don't look so frightened, darling. I will put such wicked thoughts far from me. Now smile at me with that smile that comes from heaven, and enthralls my soul. There, now tell me that you love me. Open those dear lips, and let me hear the sweetest music my ears ever listened to."

Grace strove hard to master the agitation that had overcome her as she listened to the fiery words of her lover, and looked into his clear gray eyes, now blazing with fierce passion, now melting in tenderness.

Honore!"

Her voice trembled.

"I love you with my whole soul. I am yours absolutely."

Clinton shuddered as the tender, seductive tones of her sweet voice fell upon his ear, and his eye drank in the intoxicating charm of her heavenly face, whose every feature glowed with love.

He could have cried out in a very paroxysm of passionate love.

He felt that he could not exist without the beautiful creature there before him, and no hope or fear of anything in the uncertain future could have induced him to forego her possession.

"When will you be my wife, Grace? Let it be soon. I am mad with fear when I think of the possibilities that lie between us."

"It shall be when you wish, Honore."

"You will let me fix the time?"

"Why not, Honore? You are my greatest happiness. I know your love too well to be afraid to confess that I am eager to be your wife."

"Angel!"

"Not an angel, Honore, but a woman who worships and adores you."

CHAPTER XXXI.

EVERYBODY HAPPY.

The wedding of the beautiful Grace Howard to the handsome and wealthy Marquis d'Ibberi was a great event in the upper circles of New York society.

The maidens of New York may have envied Grace, and surely the bachelors must have envied any man the possession of such a woman as Grace Howard.

The fashionable world studied the dress of the bride, and talked of her wedding gifts; commented on the bearing of the groom, and praised his magnificent presents to his bride.

Grace and her husband looked only into each other's eyes, and were happy.

They made a short wedding journey, and then returned to the city, where they intended to stay a few months before going to the home of the marquis in France.

Everybody was happy.

Grace seemed to be floating in an atmosphere of joy. She looked so distractingly sweet and matronly, her husband told her that he would some day shock the world by hugging her in public.

"And I wouldn't be to blame, Grace," he said. "You grow more lovely every day, and whenever I look at you I want to take you in my arms to assure myself that you really belong to me. If you don't look less bewitching, I shall certainly kiss you on the street, or anywhere."

"I'll look older and more dignified, then."

Grace looked as demure as a Quakeress, and Clinton pounced upon her and covered her face with kisses.

"Why," she exclaimed, laughing merrily; "it only makes you worse when I try to do better."

Yes, Grace was happy.

She showed it in every word, look, and act.

The happiness showed in the joyous light in her eyes; in the dimples that played about her merry, laughing lips; in the coming and going color in her cheeks, and in the soft, warm grasp of her little hand.

And Clinton?

He lived in the happiness of his bride.

He watched the love-light in her eyes, and fed his heart on the precious words of affection that fell from her lips.

He sought eagerly every opportunity to gratify her least whim. He told her that before they were married he had exhausted the language of love, so that no words were left to tell of the greater love that possessed him.

And Alphonse?

Ah, there was no doubt of his happiness.

After the wedding journey, Clinton had taken him quietly aside.

"Alphonse, you know I am rich."

"You have proved it to me."

Alphonse smiled pleasantly. He was thinking of the money he had borrowed of his foolish brother-in-law.

"Well, we are brothers now, and there ought to be no false delicacy between us. You know I am willing to give you as much as you ask for. Still, it must be annoying to you to have to come to me every time you want a trifle."

Alphonse wondered if he called the thousands he had borrowed trifles. He waited to hear more. The conversation pleased him.

"I have figured up my income and how much I shall need, and I find I have a surplus.

"It is not much, but if you will accept it, you are welcome. It is six thousand a year."

Even Alphonse was astonished at such generosity, and he made an exclamation to show it.

"Oh, it is nothing," said Clinton, deprecatingly. "I would gladly make it more, only I have fixed my expenses at a good figure and it only leaves this much."

"Ah," sighed Alphonse, "it is only a millionaire who can talk of such sums as trifles."

"The worst of it is"—Clinton looked troubled—"I am afraid it is not enough for you."

"Oh, D'Iberri! If I can't get along with that and my own little income together, it would be odd."

"Then it will be quite enough?"

"Plenty."

"I'm glad of that; for, you know, I could not lend you anything now."

"Don't speak of such a thing. You may be sure I'll never think of borrowing from you any more."

Of course Alphonse was happy.

Yes, they were all happy.

Even though Honore had business which took him away from his wife four or five hours each day.

He was arranging to sell some useless property, he said, so that he could purchase a home in New York.

It was not his intention to exile his wife from her native land. She should have a home in each country, and when she was tired of one place she could go to the other.

Grace smiled sweetly, and said he was her country, and that where he was she should always be happy.

"Ah, my darling, I am not so sure of that."

"Oh, Honore, you surely cannot doubt me now!"

"No, my angel, I do not doubt you, but I fear."

"Fear what?"

"Why, Grace, I can't bear to have a man look at you even; and if I consulted only my own wish, I would take you to Chateau d'Iberri, and stay there forever away from the world."

"I would be glad to go, Honore."

He shook his head.

"You think so now. But it is lonely there, and you are used to society."

There was an uneasy, troubled look in his eyes that recalled to Grace what he had once before said about his jealousy.

"Honore, darling!"

No one could have heard her tender voice, or looked into her sincere blue eyes, melting with love, without believing and adoring.

Her husband shuddered and looked away, as she continued:

"I care only for you. I shall be happiest when I am where you only can claim my attention, where upon you only can my eyes fall, where to you only can I speak. My heart is so full of love, Honore, that every day my lips could say new things, and my ears never tire of hearing you tell me of your love.

"Indeed, darling, I wish you would try me. Come, let

us go to your lovely chateau, and I will promise to pass my life there with you without a murmur, except of love and happiness, and my willingness to live only for you and with you.

"Ah, Honore, you do not know my heart if you doubt it. Come, my husband, my Honore, take me at my word."

Clinton devoured Grace with hungry looks, as in her low, sweet voice, full of passionate earnestness, she told him of her love and devotion.

He caught her in his arms, and holding her close to him, gazed into her eyes with an eager, yearning expression, as if to coax from her very soul a corroboration of her words.

"You do not doubt me, darling, do you?"

She lovingly pleaded for an answer.

"If I did doubt you, and you asked me like that to forswear myself, I could not resist. I do not doubt you, Grace, for if I did, even in so little a thing, I shudder to think of what my heart would feel."

"Then promise me that we shall go to your chateau and stay there. Oh, I promise you that you shall be the first to long for other companionship. I will be such a loving little wife, and will so cling to your heart that you will wonder you ever could fancy for one moment that I would not be satisfied with you alone."

His face lighted up.

CHAPTER XXXII.

A REMARKABLE PICTURE.

"You shall do no such penance, my sweet Grace. We will go to the chateau. If you can stay there for one year without wishing to leave it, I will promise you that after that you may have your own will."

"You promise me that?"

"I promise."

"Very well, then, sir doubter, you are likely to spend your life in your ancestral chateau. And if you catch a murmur on my lips, or detect one in my heart during that year of probation, you may—you may—let me see what you may do?"

She looked so tempting, with her rosebud lips drawn up as if in perplexity, her head held a little on one side, and her eyes half vailed by the drooping lids, that her husband exclaimed:

"I'll fix the punishment and inflict it now."

She did not object to the punishment, seemingly, for when her lips were free, she saucily said:

"Have you only one mode of punishment?"

Clinton turned hastily away, and looking out of the window, answered, hoarsely:

"Fifty."

She laughed merrily.

"Then it is agreed. One year of probation. When shall we start? I am ready now."

"I must finish my business here first. Then off we go, eh?"

"Off we go. And see who tires first."

The Marquis d'Iberri was never very precise about the details of his business affairs, and never told anybody where he transacted them.

It is true that nobody asked any questions, for the only person who had the right to ask was Grace, and she seemed to care only that Honore was with her again when he had been away.

It was an odd way to go about selling and buying property, and if he had not said it was what he was engaged in, no person who had taken the trouble to follow him would have believed it was what he was doing.

When he had taken leave of Grace with as much affection as if he had not expected to see her again for a twelve-month, the marquis would walk down town some distance, turn into an unfrequented side-street, walk along it to another street, and so on, turning and turning until he stood in front of a quiet-looking house.

Now, if anybody were following him, in spite of his great care to be unobserved, and should come up and look him in the face, that person would be chagrined to discover that it was not the marquis at all, but another person.

The man who would stand a moment in front of the house and then enter it would be a brown-bearded young fellow, not unlike the Clinton Hastings who once painted pictures in Morlaix, in Upper Britanny.

Call him Clinton Hastings.

Walking up stairs as if he had the right to do so, Clinton would stop before a door, fit a key into its lock, open it, and walk in.

The room, it would be found, was fitted like a studio, and Clinton, it would be seen, was at his old work of painting pictures.

In the autumn the artists of New York have an exhibition to show their work, and fashionable people always go to the exhibition.

The autumn before the marquis and his wife went to the Chateau d'Iberri, there was the usual exhibition, and on the opening night everybody of any consequence was there.

Grace was fond of pictures, and she went for that reason, and the marquis went because his wife wished to go.

The marquis knew very little about art, but he told Grace that if she only would tell him when to admire, she should have no reason to be ashamed of him.

Most fashionable folks go on opening night to see and be seen, and so it was crowded, this opening night at the Academy.

It was hard work to have an opportunity to see the pictures, what with the friends who wished to say "how do you do?" to a real marquis, and with the crowds who cared very little what they said so that they said something.

A few there were who went to see the pictures, and one of these, meeting Grace and her husband, went into rhapsodies over a life-size painting of extraordinary merit by an unknown artist.

It hung in the north room, where comparatively few people were, and more for that reason than to see that especial picture Grace asked to be taken there.

"Be sure to tell me if I am to admire it, Grace."

Grace answered by a loving smile and a pressure of the arm she was leaning on.

Any little jest of Honore's made her happy.

A number of persons were grouped together, all looking at one large picture, evidently the one in question.

They took up a position to get a fair view of the picture.

Its title was "False Vows and False Faces."

It represented a blindfolded man and a masked woman.

The woman, standing on tiptoe, had her hands on the

man's shoulders, while he was bent over a little to receive the kiss which her upturned face seemed about to offer.

His face was full of eager expectancy; hers, covered by the mask, could not be seen.

She was marvelously beautiful in figure.

"Is it good, Grace?"

They had looked at it a few moments in silence.

Grace spoke never a word.

Her eyes were fixed upon the picture in a gaze of stony horror.

Her sweet face was livid and agonized.

"Why, Grace, my darling, what is it?" whispered her husband, in terrified tones.

"Save me!" gasped Grace. "Save me from him. Take me away."

She turned to her husband in a piteous appeal, and sank lifeless in his arms.

All that night Grace tossed moaning in her bed.

Now sleeping, pursued by frightened dreams; now waking and clinging to Honore, who slept peacefully through it all.

When morning came and Honore asked her how she had passed the night, she made no answer, but laid her head upon his shoulder and sobbed as if her heart would break.

"Poor little Grace," he said, soothingly, "You have had too much gayety lately. You need rest. Let us go to our old-fashioned home in dear old France, and there you will be away from all this turmoil.

"My dear little bird! Ah! how frightened I was when you fell into my arms so limp and lifeless. I thought I had lost my Grace and I was nearly crazy; but they said it was only the heat that had made you faint. There, now, calm yourself, my darling, and——"

"And you will take me to your home, Honore?"

She interrupted him, eagerly looking up at him with her tear-stained face, beseechingly as a little child.

"You will, won't you, dear?"

She nestled closer to him.

"And you will see how contented and well and happy I shall be. I shall indeed, Honore, dear."

"Poor, dear little Grace! We will go at once on the first steamer."

He tenderly smoothed the golden hair with his hand.

"Talk to me, Honore," she said, suddenly. "Tell me about the chateau."

"Tell you about the chateau? To me it is beautiful. It has nothing modern about it. Even the furniture is old. But you won't mind that, will you?"

"Not with you there, Honore. If I have you, that is all."

"I am glad of that. I was afraid you might wish me to change the furniture."

"Never, Honore! If you like it best so, that is enough for me. I only want you, Honore."

It was pitiful to see how she returned to that idea, as if she were fearful he might be taken from her.

He noticed it, and tried to reassure her.

"Well, you have me, my Grace. Have me as securely as the honest vows of an honest man and an honest woman and the laws of France and America can bind us."

"Yes, yes, Honore, I know I have you; but I love you so, darling, that if anything should—but you will always love me, won't you, my hus—my Honore, my true love, my everything?"

She would have said her husband, but the word seemed to sting her, for she started up, and concluded her words, passionately clinging to him.

CHAPTER XXXIII.

WHO PAINTED THE PICTURE?

Honore would not have left Grace at all that day, had she not insisted upon it, declaring that she was much better.

No sooner had her husband left the house, than, with feverish haste, she sought Alphonse.

"Are you sure that Clinton Hastings is dead?"

"Hello! What's up now?"

"Tell me, tell me! Are you sure?"

Grace nervously pulled at her handkerchief.

"Why, of course, I'm sure. As sure as anybody can be. But what on earth is the matter now?"

"Have you been to the Academy yet?"

"Certainly; I was there last night."

"Did you see that picture in the north room?"

"What picture? What is the matter with you, Grace? Anything turned up about Hastings?"

"There's a picture in the north gallery of a blindfolded man, who looks like the artist, and a woman in a mask, dressed exactly as I was that night."

"Well, what of it?"

"What of it? Suppose he should have painted it?"

"If he's dead, how could he? Do be sensible, Grace."

"But if he's not dead?"

"He is dead, I tell you; but, even if he were not, it needn't make any difference to you, as long as he doesn't find you out."

"What!"

Grace drew herself up proudly.

"Much as I love Honore, sure as I am it would kill me to leave him, if I thought Clinton Hastings was alive, I would confess everything."

Grace buried her face in her hands, and rocked to and fro, sobbing piteously.

Alphonse was alarmed.

Not at the disgrace which hung over his sister, but at the danger which threatened himself.

The danger of his having his six thousand a year withdrawn.

"You surely would do no such silly thing, Grace?"

"Alphonse," she sobbed, "if Clinton Hastings were alive, Honore would not be my husband. Oh, my brother, help me!"

"What can I do? Don't I tell you the artist is dead? He was killed that very night."

"But who else could paint the picture? Who else could have known the details?"

"A mere coincidence. But I'll tell you what I'll do, Grace. I'll go see the directors, and pretend I want to buy the picture. In that way I can see the artist."

"Do, Alphonse. Go now. Right away, that's a good brother."

Not because he was a good brother, but because he was so intensely selfish, Alphonse set out, determined to bring back such a report as would satisfy Grace, and turn her from her project of confessing to D'Iberri that she had already been married.

He first went to the Academy and looked at the picture. He could not avoid a start of fear.

"This is not a coincidence," he murmured; "and yet how can Hastings be alive? Bah! even if he is, he cannot have any suspicion of who we are. I will make sure."

Inquiry of one of the directors brought out the address, but not the name of the artist.

Alphonse hastened to the address and was shortly knocking at the door of the studio where we have once before been.

"Come in."

Alphonse entered.

The artist turned with a smile of inquiry.

Alphonse gasped and turned pale.

Clinton Hastings sat before him.

Sat there almost as he had once before sat in the studio in the lowly house in Morlaix, before the masked man.

Alphonse recovered himself in a moment.

It was quite evident that Clinton Hastings did not suspect him.

"I have come to see you, sir, about your famous painting in the Academy."

Clinton smiled.

"You are the tenth this morning. I am much flattered that my painting is successful, but it is not for sale."

"Ah! I am sorry for that. I had set my heart on having it. I believe in encouraging American artists."

"Oh, I'll take the encouragement without the money."

Alphonse recognized the mockery which once before had driven him nearly to despair. He only smiled, however.

"It is an odd subject for a painting."

"I am sure it must be. The other nine gentlemen who called this morning to encourage me said the same thing."

Alphonse bit his lip.

"I am afraid you do not like criticism."

"Were you criticising? How stupid of me not to recognize the fact."

"Stupid or discourteous! I don't know which," retorted Alphonse, angrily.

"Sir," said Clinton, in the same mocking tone, "are your eyes in good working order?"

"I do not understand you."

"No? I thought the question simple enough. However, I will put it in another way.   Can you see that window distinctly?"

A startled expression crept into Alphonse's eyes.

" "Yes," he replied, with a poor attempt at a smile.

"That is very odd, then."

" What is very odd?"

" Why, that you should use such language to me when you know there is a window handy."

Clinton's smile was as mocking and his tone as airy and careless as ever it had been.

Alphonse was ghastly.

" I do not understand," he stammered.

" That is not strange, *ami*, it is so long ago that we talked of windows."

This was said in French.

Alphonse gasped, looked wildly at Clinton a moment, and then turned and fled down stairs, pursued by the mocking laugh of the artist.

CHAPTER XXXIV.

ALPHONSE YEARNS FOR FRANCE.

When Alphonse reached the street, he walked hurriedly to the corner, turned, saw he was not followed, and then walked aimlessly about for a full half-hour.

It was evident to him that he was known, and it was as certain that the artist must know about Grace.   If he had not known all he cared to know, he would certainly have followed him.

What was to be done?

For his own sake, he must keep this fact from Grace.

He might do it for a time, but how long, must, of course, depend upon the will of the artist.

Could he in any way rid himself of the artist?

Now he regretted the death of Caradoc.

And yet Caradoc had deceived him before.

Ah, if he could only do it himself!

But how?

No, it would not do.   It was too dangerous.

If he only had him in Paris!

There he knew the haunts of the desperadoes, and could get one to do the thing for him.

Why, yes, he could persuade D'Iberri to hasten his departure.

Perhaps the artist would follow.

If he did, all would be well. If he did not, it would be better.

Full of this idea, he hastened back to Grace, and assured her that he had seen the artist, who had told him that the scene was taken from an old English play.

And as for the artist himself, Alphonse declared he was as unlike Hastings as was possible.

Anxious to be reassured, Grace was induced to believe this story with very little difficulty.

Nevertheless she could not overcome the shock she had received, and was determined to urge Honore to take her at once to his home, where she could feel free from any chance of similar untoward occurrences.

She told Alphonse of her intention, and he warmly applauded the idea that fell in so well with his own wishes.

He sought Honore at the first convenient moment that evening, and told very pathetically of how anxious Grace was to be in her own home in beautiful France.

And Honore assured him that if they could be ready in time, the steamer of three days later should take them.

"You will come with us, will you not, Alphonse?"

"I will go as far as Paris, anyhow. I don't know about burying myself in the country."

"Giddy fellow!" exclaimed Honore, smiling.

The three days that followed were anxious ones to Alphonse, who expected at any moment to hear the mocking laugh or the jeering voice of the artist.

He haunted the house in his fear lest Grace might by some means learn of her husband's existence.

What did he care for her scruples.

He did not even pretend to himself any other anxiety than the real one. He did not propose to lose his comfortable income if he could help it.

Neither his sister's honor and happiness, nor the artist's life, should stand in the way of his pleasures.

Grace passed the time in a condition of unrest totally unlike her usual sweet composure.

The shock she had received had made her timid and fearful.

She believed Alphonse, but the picture kept coming up

before her all the time, and she could not get rid of the idea
that something might occur to make the incident of her life
known to Honore.

She did not mean to deceive him. She had all along intended to tell him about it before her marriage; but she
had put it off until he had told her so vehemently that he
could not brook the idea that she could ever have loved or
caressed another.

Then she felt that she could not speak.

She could not lose the love of this man who was so tender
and true, so brave and frank.

She had been glad, positively glad when she had thought
that she might die with him—die without having to tell her
secret.

She would have been happy could she have told him
everything; but the recollection of the fierce passion he had
once displayed sealed her lips.

The thought of losing his love almost made her frantic.

She followed him about the house, clinging to him as if
she could not let him be away from her.

He soothed and petted her; humoring her every whim,
and doing all he could to reassure her.

He talked to her of the old chateau, and told her how
happy they should be there.

Free to do as they wished. Nobody to please but themselves.

"You will live for me, my Grace, and I for you. You
must be happy there, darling, for my heart is set upon it."

"Do not fear, Honore," she replied. "I shall love the
chateau if you are in it. I want to get away from here and
be where you can be by my side all the time. Will you tire
of that, dear?"

"Tire of it? Come, I'll wager a kiss you will be the first
to tire."

"I'll wager and pay in advance, so you will have two to
pay in case you lose, as you surely will."

CHAPTER XXXV.

IN FRANCE AMONG OLD FRIENDS.

Each member of the little party had some special cause
of gratification in the fact of being once more in France.

"MON DIEU! YOU HERE?"   "I, OR MY GHOST; AND I THINK IT IS I."—(P. 16.)

Honore was happy because Grace had gradually been recovering her former cheerful spirits, and was now quite herself again.

Grace was happy because she was now almost in the secluded spot where, with her idol, she might hope for perfect peace from intrusion and trouble.

Alphonse was happy because he knew the artist had not come on the same steamer, anyhow, and it would make very little difference if he should come later, for he hoped to have Grace and D'Iberri out of Paris in a few days.

They did not go at once, however, for Honore had considerable to do looking after neglected business affairs, and Grace was occupied not unpleasantly in meeting many old friends.

Alphonse plunged at once into all the dissipations of which he was so fond, and of which Paris offered him such a plenty.

The days went by so free from any sign of Hastings that Alphonse had almost forgotten him.

One evening he was having a good time at a cafe concert, ogling the women in approved Parisian style, and joking boisterously with his friends, when some one tapped him on the shoulder.

" *Bon soir, ami.* "

It was Clinton's mocking salutation.

" *Mon Dieu!* You here?"

" I, or my ghost; and between ourselves, I think it is I, for I am very sure I am not dead *yet.* "

" What do you want?"

" Ah, *mon Dieu!* what memories that question awakes. Do you remember, *mon ami,* how I asked you that question one night nearly four years ago? Ah! I shall never forget that; your answer was so witty."

Alphonse had drawn him one side so that their conversation should not be overheard.

" What do you want?"

" That was not just as I put it, you will remember. I said:

" ' Which shall it be, my money or my life?'

" And you answered, so wittily:

" ' If I wanted the one I would not come here; if I wanted the other I would wait a few days.' "

" Will you tell me why you have come here to see me?"

"Certainly. But I can't help thinking of that night. Do you remember how you wanted to postpone the episode of the window? Dear me! how delightful it is to go over old times, isn't it?"

"If you do not tell me your business with me I shall rejoin my friends."

"Why, if you are really in such a hurry, I suppose I must let you go. *Bon soir.* I thought maybe I could tell you what I had to say on the way home; but it will do when you join us."

There was a hidden meaning in this speech that made Alphonse uneasy. He said:

"Join you—where?"

"At home, of course. You'll be home by and by, won't you?"

"Home! What home?"

"Oh, there, now, don't quibble over terms. A hotel isn't home, of course, exactly, but I always call home any place where my wife is."

"Your wife!"

"Yes. Why, what's the matter with you, Alphonse? Have you forgotten that I married your sister, Grace?"

The artist laughed in his peculiarly diabolical way, and Alphonse felt as if he could strangle him then and there.

It was evidently useless to resist. He must in some way gain time, and, in the meantime, there was nothing for it but to submit.

He put aside all attempt at pretense of ignorance, and with a laugh he endeavored to make careless, he said:

"I'll give in. Wait till I excuse myself, and I will follow you."

"Always the same obliging fellow, dear brother."

"I'll oblige you yet," murmured Alphonse, under his breath, as he went toward his friends and bade them adieu.

When they were in the street, Clinton turned to him.

"*Mon ami!* disagreeable as it may be to you to recall old memories, I must for a moment take you back to that November night when I made the gentle, loving Grace, my wife. You offered me twenty thousand francs then."

"Ten thousand, if you please."

"Oh, well, we will not quarrel over a trifle; say twenty thousand. I refused the money then. I'll take it now."

"Oho," thought Alphonse, it is money he wants. I see my way clear now."

Then aloud:

"But if I have not the money now?"

"It will suit me just as well. I thought I'd ask you, that's all. I can get it elsewhere. *Au revoir.* Sorry to have given you any trouble."

"Hold on. I didn't say I did not have it."

"Oh, no; but I understood you would have to borrow it of D'Iberri, and, if it comes to that, I might as well do it myself, bless you! He'd give it to me for Grace's sake. Dear Grace!"

"You shall have the twenty thousand francs."

"How much did you say?"

"Twenty thousand."

"Did it sound like twenty?"

"It did."

"Now, that's odd, isn't it? Have you ever noticed how easy it is to make mistakes? I—well, I won't say I said thirty, but that's the sum, dear brother."

"You will ruin me."

"No, no, brother dear, don't say that. Come, let me go to D'Iberri, to Honore. He will have it."

"Devil!"

"Ha! ha! Do you remember how I thought you must be the devil that night? Funny how things come about, isn't it?"

"Will you give me a week to get the money in?"

Alphonse was choking with rage at the thought of being so played with; but he was powerless for the moment.

"A week. Well, all right. Bring it to me, please, at No. 27 Rue d'Artois, third floor. Always high up, you see. That's on account of the windows, you know. More convenient to drop things, or people, out of. *Au revoir.*"

Clinton's mocking laugh rang with a hateful echo in Alphonse's ear, and he could have torn the bitter tongue from the artist's mouth with his own hands.

"You may laugh now," he muttered, "but it will be my turn before long."

CHAPTER XXXVI.

OLD AND NEW ACQUAINTANCES.

"Robert, you are a fool!"

The speaker was a woman. A rare type of the sensuous beauty of the south of France.

Full, red lips; clear olive skin, with the rich blood glowing underneath; dark-brown eyes; heavy jet-black hair; a tiny, piquant nose; rather heavy, well-arched eyebrows; low forehead; small, regular teeth, gleaming white behind the full lips.

A medium height, plump contour, serpent-like grace of motion.

Now lazy and languid of speech; now quick and full of fire.

It was with a lazy drawl that she complimented Robert, who, indeed, was none other than our old friend Tete-de-Fer.

"Call me so if you will, Elise," answered Tete-de-Fer, with more graciousness than one would have believed such a brute capable of. But I tell you that Bras-de-Fer is the devil. If I do it, he will know."

"Bah! And are you to starve because your Bras-de-Fer is not here to say help yourself?"

"Elise, he would think no more of choking me to death than he would of eating an oyster alive. Wait; you will see him some day, and you, too, will agree that he must be obeyed. He said to me, '*Mon ami*, do not touch him!' and not even for you, Elise, will I do it."

"As you please, Robert," said the woman, contemptuously. "But when I leave you for some one who can give me what I ask for, do not howl like a wild beast and talk of love."

"You would not dare, Elise."

His eyes blazed with jealous fury.

"Dare!"

The woman spoke quickly now, and she looked like a tigress.

" Dare! When you tell me something Elise Candolet does not dare, then talk. Bah! You once had a heart of iron, but since you met your wonderful Bras-de-Fer you have exchanged it for a chicken's."

" What's the use of being cross, Elise? I tell you, you don't know him."

Tete-de-Fer was almost as submissive before this woman he adored as he was before Bras-de-Fer whom he feared.

" He is a man, isn't he, and only a man? Did you ever see a man who would say what I should or should not do?"

" That is because you are so beautiful, Elise. All men must do as you bid."

" Fah! You make me sick. Beauty! I know I have it; but it is not that men are afraid of. It's my claws and my teeth. Men look at me, and know I will scratch and bite deep."

" You can be fearful, Elise."

Tete-de-Fer spoke admiringly.

" Ah! And you pretend, maybe, you do as I tell you from love. I do not say you do not love; but it is fear—Robert, fear—that makes you do my will. Love! *Ciel!* If you only loved me, you would beat me. I know you, Robert; and I tell you, you must ask that young French-American for more money, or I will leave you."

" And I will kill you if you do."

" If you can."

" I could strangle.you now as I would a baby; you are not Bras-de-Fer."

" Do it."

She threw back her head, as if inviting him, but her hand clutched something in the folds of her dress, and her brown eyes were black in their rage.

Tete-de-Fer laughed uneasily.

" I was only joking."

" Liar! You do not dare lay a finger on me! You know what it would cost you."

" Now, what's the use, Elise," he said, coaxingly, " to get into a tantrum? Maybe I was mistaken about the man."

" Don't play the fool with me, Robert. It was the man. There you stand, with a scar on your ribs now, of his making, and you talk to me of your Bras-de-Fer! I swear to you—and you know if I keep my oaths—that, if

you do not bring me some money—five thousand francs—
this night, I will leave you!"

" But if——"

" No 'but ifs.' I have said it."

" All right, Elise. I will do it; but I know Bras-de-Fer,
and you do not."

" Bah! If your Bras-de-Fer turns up, bring him to me,
and we shall see if he can scare me."

" When shall I go?"

" *Mon Dieu!* Go now, now, now!"

Tete-de-Fer opened the door.

" I will go, but——"

" How many buts you make."

" Give me a kiss, then."

" Not a kiss till I have the money."

" *Au revoir*, then. Ah! *mon Dieu!* He here!"

" Why, yes, *ami*. I am here. Why not? What more
natural? Introduce me to your sister—that sweet, pretty,
loving sister, of whom you have told me so little, and I
know so much."

" Eh! *mon Dieu!* Who is this, then, that comes unan-
nounced into people's rooms?"

There was a dangerous flash in the brown eyes.

Elise guessed in a moment that the cool, easy-going intruder was the Bras-de-Fer, of whom she had heard so
much.

She surveyed him with an angry stare.

He gazed at her with an air in which curiosity, amusement, impudence, indifference, and admiration were provokingly mingled.

The warm, southern blood flushed her cheeks, and the
brown eyes blazed.

Passion was quick and vehement with Elise. She had
already hated the man for his power over Tete-de-Fer.

Now she hated him for his cool and easy assumption of
power.

She would show him.

" This is my apartment. Get out."

The round throat swelled like a cobra's, almost, and the
shapely little hand pointing to the door fairly quivered with
the transport of rage.

" I don't know if I like you best so, or when you are more
languid. Beautiful anyhow."

Bras-de-Fer spoke with the cool unconcern of a critic, and eyed the angry woman, with head on one side, as if examining a statue.

Tete-de-Fer, somewhat angry, somewhat awed, somewhat curious, silently watched to see which of his superiors would come off victor.

Elise emitted a low, stifled shriek of rage.

This man dared to laugh at her.

"Out, out!"

She could hardly speak the words.

The outstretched arm waved passionately toward the door and a foot stamped vehement emphasis on the floor.

"Yes, on the whole, I like you best so. Very beautiful, indeed."

The nervous little hand sought the pocket.

A bound, a flash.

A little dagger cut the air, and——

A low laugh from Bras-de-Fer.

The woman sat on the lounge.

"Poisoned, eh?"

Bras-de-Fer examined the glistening steel.

"Yes, it's poisoned. Madam, accept my sincerest homage. You and I shall be able to do good work together. I have looked for just such a woman a long time. I'm glad I have found you at last. It's all right, *ami*."

Turning to Tete-de-Fer.

"No need for jealousy. Loving is out of my line. I merely wanted such a woman, and——"

He looked calmly at the furious creature he had forced to sit down.

"I have found her."

Tete-de-Fer stared from one to the other.

He accepted what Bras-de-Fer said, just as he said it. He had told Elise she did not know him. Now she did.

And Elise?

Bras-de-Fer had laughed at her fury.

She had struck her fangs at him.

He had still laughed.

She looked at this man again.

She knew within herself that this man was her master. Woman-like, she accepted the situation.

Woman-like, she did not say so.

"Some other time," she said.

Bras-de-Fer no longer smiled provokingly. He smiled in admiration now. He tendered her the dagger again.

"Elise, you are one woman in a million. Nobody can use this as well as you. Take it, and take with it the homage of a man who has never come so near failing to conquer a human being. Forgive me if I have succeeded with you. It was a harder struggle than it seemed. Will you give me your hand?"

She was completely conquered.

She put her hand in his.

Tete-de-Fer was crazy with jealousy.

Yet he dared not say a word.

CHAPTER XXXVII.

ARRANGING FOR A FUNERAL.

"This is my friend Bras-de-Fer. He has something to say to you."

"Right in here, messieurs—in here."

"Stay outside, Monsieur Caradoc. If I wish you I will send for you."

In nowise offended at such a disposal of him, Tete-de-Fer sat in the main room of the low cabaret, while Bras-de-Fer and the landlord, a tall, white-bearded, asthmatic old rascal, went into an inner room.

"Now, monsieur," said Bras-de-Fer, abruptly, "see if I know you well. You would sell your own mother if you got a good price—is it not so?"

"Monsieur!"

The old man spoke indignantly.

"Oh, well, I s'pose you have no mother; but if you had you would sell her. Come, no nonsense. Is there anything you would not do for a thousand francs?"

"That depends."

A very expressive shrug of the shoulders.

"Depends upon the danger I suppose?"

"Exactly."

"Good! There is no danger in this."

"What must I do?"

"Remain in that room," pointing to an adjoining room, "until I let you out."

"And what will you do?"

"That is not your business."

"But I must know."

"You must not. Come! I offer you one thousand francs to stay one hour in that room. Will you say yes? Quick!"

"Monsieur must know that there are many men who come here who do not wish to be seen or known, and——"

"Bah! You mean that escaped convicts, men wanted, and thieves, murderers, etcetera, come here; and that you must be on hand all the time. I know that and have provided for it. Will you take my offer? I am in a hurry. Quick!"

"Monsieur can see."

"I can see you are an old fool, and that it is useless to reason with you; therefore——"

Bras-de-Fer, with a combined coolness and dexterity that would have done credit to the most accomplished garroter, caught the old man by the neck, and had gagged him before he could utter more than the faintest sound.

Then he bound him securely and carried him into the next room, where he stowed him comfortably away under a bed.

Having done this he drew from his pocket a wig and false whiskers.

He then took off his eyebrows, and various other peculiar features, which made the difference between Bras-de-Fer and Clinton Hastings.

The wig and whiskers were put on, and paint and other disguising agents were used, and monsieur, the landlord, appeared where Bras-de-Fer had but just stood.

Bras-de-Fer had evidently studied his make-up in advance of his visit.

He passed out into the main room and took his place behind the bar.

He beckoned to Tete-de Fer.

"Do you answer for this friend of yours, this Bras-de-Fer?"

Never doubting it was the landlord who spoke, Tete-de-Fer answered unhesitatingly.

"Certainly. Why?"

"Because I suspect him for a detective. Is he?"

Tete-de-Fer stammeringly denied that his friend was any such thing.

But the other shook his head.

"I am sure he is, and I suppose he has deceived you. I was so sure that when I got him inside I drugged him and took off his false eyebrows and whiskers. He is in there now, tied well."

"And drugged?"

Tete-de-Fer spoke eagerly.

"Drugged. Sound asleep. He is a detective. Will you do him?"

"Ah!"

There was a fierce joy in the man's tone.

" Take me to him?"

"First tell me will you do him?"

"Gladly as I would a dog."

"One would think you hated him."

"Hate him! Take me to him. He has played with me, as he would with a child, and made me do his bidding. Take me to him."

Inwardly laughing, Clinton led the way into the inner room.

"Now promise me you will kill him."

"I will kill him though I die the next minute."

"Is your knife ready?"

Tete-de-Fer drew it from an inner pocket.

"Ho, ho!" laughed Clinton, in the tone of Bras-de-Fer. "How you must hate me, indeed, poor Robert."

The ferocious expression of Tete-de-Fer's face passed into one of amazement, and from that into one of sheepish chagrin.

"I wanted to try my disguise, *ami*," said Clinton; so put up your knife for the present. You may find an opportunity to use it on me some day, but not yet."

And Clinton laughed in his mocking way.

"Now let us return and wait for our friend. You go first. I would be afraid to have you behind me just now."

Again Clinton laughed, and Tete-de-Fer ground his teeth in silent rage.

They had not been in the main room long before Alphonse, in a very thin disguise, entered the cabaret. He went at once to the bar and spoke to the landlord.

"I want to see you alone for a few minutes."

"Yes, monsieur. Will monsieur come into this little room? Now monsieur can talk without fear of listeners."

"There are one thousand francs. I want you to find me a man I can depend upon."

Clinton made a pretense of eagerly pocketing the money.

"What does monsieur want the man for? Is it for a— that is, do you want him to arrange a funeral for you? Eh? He, he!"

"It is for that," exactly."

The answer was as calm as if it was only the life of a chicken that was in question.

"A funeral, eh? Let me see. Will to-morrow night do, or must you have him to-night?"

"To-night, if possible."

"I can give you the address of a man, if you like. He does not come here, because he has made some enemies on account of a funeral he arranged only a short time ago."

"Is he a sure man?"

"Never fails."

"Give me his address."

"Ask for Bras-de-Fer, No. 150 Rue d'Argent."

Alphonse left without ceremony, and a few moments later Bras-de-Fer and Tete-de-Fer followed, the landlord having been released and afterward mollified by a present of the thousand francs left by Alphonse.

Dismissing Tete-de-Fer, Clinton hurried to the room he had taken in Rue d'Argent, and arrived there sufficiently long before Alphonse to be ready to receive him.

He was lying on a lounge, smoking a vile cigar, when a rap sounded on the door.

"Come in," he shouted.

Alphonse entered.

Bras-de-Fer sprang to his feet and pointed a pistol at him.

"Well, who are you? What do you want? Quick!"

Alphonse smiled.

"I have business for you."

Still the pistol pointed at him.

"Put that thing away; I am from old Daddy Braune."

Bras-de-Fer lowered the pistol slowly, as if his suspicions were only half allayed.

"And what does he want of me?"

"He says you know how to arrange a funeral for me."

"Ah! And you. Who are you?"

"What does that matter so that I pay you well?"

"How much will you pay?"

"How much do you want?"

"I don't want anything. Good-night, monsieur."

"Oh, come! I will pay you five thousand francs."

"Five thousand thunders! Say twenty thousand, and it's done; say less, and you waste breath."

"It is a high price."

"It is my price. Good-night."

"I will give it."

"Good! And who is the man, and how shall I find him? Tell me everything."

"His name is Clinton Hastings. He lives at No. 27 Rue d'Artois."

"Good!"

"He is an artist. He is expecting me to send him some money this week. I will give you the money, and you can——"

"Do as I please with it. Good. Give me the money."

"Yes, friend Bras-de-Fer, after the deed is done. It will not be so easy, for he is a powerful man."

"Very well, monsieur. Good-night."

"You will do it then?"

"I will *not* do it."

"How? Not do it?"

"Not until you give me the money first."

"But—well, never mind. I will give you half first, and the other half afterward."

"All or nothing."

"But you may fail."

Bras-de-Fer laughed boisterously.

"I never fail."

"But suppose——"

"Suppose I should take your money and not do your work. Suppose it if you like. Ask Daddy Braune if I work that way. I did not seek you. You came to me. My terms are cash in advance. If you don't like them go elsewhere."

Alphonse studied the brutal face and muscular proportions of Bras-de-Fer, and decided.

"I will bring you the money to-morrow night."

"Yes, and I know how you will get it," said Bras-de-Fer, when he had closed the door on Alphonse.

CHAPTER XXXVIII.

ALPHONSE STUDIES THE BANKING SYSTEM.

The next morning Alphonse entered the room where the Marquis d'Iberri sat making out checks.

"Ah!" exclaimed Alphonse, carelessly; "balancing your accounts, I suppose?"

"No. I never do that. It is too much trouble. When I run short at the bank they let me know. I ought to look over my checks at the end of the month, but I never do."

"I should think that would be dangerous."

"Why dangerous?"

"Because if anybody should forge your signature well enough to pass the bank, you would never find it out."

"Oh, come now, Alphonse, you can't scare me into better business habits. I know I'm careless, but I'm not going to take the trouble of overhauling my checks every month on the chance of finding a forgery."

Alphonse laughed pleasantly.

"I wouldn't either if I were you," he said.

The marquis continued making out checks, tearing them from his check-book, and pushing them hastily into a pile at one side of his desk.

Alphonse had taken up a book, and while pretending to read it, was all the time watching his brother-in-law.

Presently a maid came and told the marquis that Grace wished to see him.

"I'll be gone about fifteen minutes, Alphonse. Will you be here that long?"

"I guess so."

"Well, then, I won't take the trouble to lock these things up."

The marquis hastened away.

Alphonse listened intently until he heard the marquis shut the door of Grace's room.

Then he crept softly to the desk, and hastily ran over the checks.

"Ah!" he muttered. "Here's one for a thousand, payable to bearer. It will be easier to alter that than to risk a signature."

With these words he slipped the check from the pile, and placed it in the waste-basket under some torn bits of paper.

"There! Now if he misses it and makes a fuss about it, I'll help him find it."

Alphonse was in his seat, buried in his book, when the marquis returned.

Merely glancing at his brother-in-law, the marquis wrote a few more checks and closed the check-book.

Then he took a pile of bills and commenced sorting them, putting with each one a check to pay it with.

Alphonse watched him stealthily.

Finally the marquis'took a bill and searched vainly among the checks for the one to pay it.

"Hum!" he muttered, half-aloud. "I thought I had made a check for this; but, I suppose, I didn't."

Thereupon he opened his check-book again, and made out another check.

Alphonse heaved a sigh of relief.

"We are going to D'Iberri in a week, Alphonse," said the marquis, as he arose to go. "I suppose you won't go with us."

"No, I thank you. Paris is good enough for me."

When the marquis had left the room, Alphonse picked the check out of the basket, and placing it in his pocket, went to his room and locked himself in.

Later in the day he presented himself at the bank, and handed in a check for twenty-one thousand francs.

The teller being accustomed to paying checks to Alphonse, handed him the money without a word.

During the afternoon the marquis, with a troubled expression on his face, hurried into the bank, and asked to see the cashier in private.

When they were alone together the marquis exhibited the most profound grief, and seemed with difficulty to command himself enough to say:

"Monsieur, I come to you, not only as to the manager of this institution, but as to a man of honor in whom I have confidence."

"Why, my lord, what can have happened?"

"Alas! such a misfortune! I hardly have the courage to tell you."

"Have you met with losses in speculation?"

"If that were all, I would be happy. No, my millions are untouched. I fear—but tell me, monsieur, have any of my checks been cashed to-day?"

"I will see."

The cashier went out, and returned in a few moments with half a dozen checks.

"Are they all genuine?" asked the marquis.

The cashier carefully scanned them.

"Yes."

"Thank Heaven! Then I may be mistaken. Let me see them."

He looked them over, and suddenly started.

"May I ask who presented this one for twenty-one thousand?"

The cashier went out and asked the paying-teller.

"Monsieur Gorinot," he said, when he returned to the marquis.

The latter uttered a groan, and buried his face in his hands.

"Oh, my poor wife! If she should ever learn of this! Monsieur," he continued, turning to the startled cashier, "this is an altered check. Look closely and you will see. I made it out for one thousand francs, and it was stolen from my desk while I was out of the room. Oh, monsieur, advise me. What shall I do?"

"He ought to be arrested."

"Oh, no, no. I do not care for him, but my poor wife! The ingrate! Why, monsieur, I gave him thirty thousand francs a year, and yet he steals from me."

"Marquis, the cashier spoke, sternly, "justice demands that such a rascal should be punished."

"Yes, monsieur, yes," said the marquis, sadly, "but think of my poor wife, who is an angel."

"But it is my duty, marquis, to inform against him."

"Listen, monsieur. It will kill my wife, and if you inform against him you will punish my wife and me. This is the first offense, remember."

"Yes, but in these cases the first is soon followed. I know your brother-in-law. He is very dissipated, and if he finds this passes unnoticed he will try it again."

The marquis was silent for several minutes. At last he spoke.

"Monsieur, it must not be. At least let me try to reform him. For my innocent wife's sake let this pass."

The earnestness of the marquis deeply affected the upright cashier.

"I consent then for this time."

"You must do more than that."

"How! More?"

"Yes, monsieur. I know that Alphonse will resort to forgery. I am sure of it, but I feel that I can reform him in time. What I wish to do is to leave fifty thousand francs with you as a fund against his forged checks. If I do not reform him before that is gone I will let the law take its course."

This seemed a strange way to go about reforming a forger, and the cashier at first refused to accede to the plan, but was finally persuaded when the marquis promised not to interfere if the effort at reform should fail.

The marquis left the bank, grief written in every line of his face, but when he was in his carriage the grief gave way to grim satisfaction.

"I think I have paved the way for your punishment, my murdering, forging brother-in-law."

CHAPTER XXXIX.

A HARD MAN TO KILL.

"Good-day, monsieur. Have you the money?"

It was Bras-de-Fer who spoke, Alphonse who answered.

"Yes. Count it."

Bras-de-Fer slowly counted and carefully examined the notes.

"Right. When can I see your man?"

"To-night if you wish. He is at home, for I came that way, and inquired."

"Good. There will be a funeral without mourners."

"You will not fail?"

"Diable! I tell you I never fail."

"But he is a powerful man."

"And I? Look!"

"Bras-de-Fer took up a heavy poker and bent it double without any seeming effort.

"Why else am I called Iron-Arm? Bah! Listen. You want to know how I will do it?"

"Monsieur Hastings, here is your money from—who shall I say sends it?"

"The man of the black mask."

"Good. Monsieur Hastings, here is your money from the man of the black mask.

"I throw it on the table. Some of it falls on the floor. Like that. See?

"He stoops to pick it up. I——"

He drew a long, sharp dirk-knife from his coat, and made a rapid lunge, as if into the back of a stooping man.

"He says 'oh!' That is all.

"Ho, ho! You could do it yourself another time."

Even Alphonse was sickened at the sight of the gleeful brutality of Bras-de-Fer, and waiting only to caution him to be very careful, he hurried away.

That night Alphonse was nervous, but he drowned that in wine.

The next night he was happy because the morning papers had told of the murder of an American artist at No. 27 Rue d'Artois.

Alphonse celebrated his release by an orgy begun in one of his favorite cafe-concerts, and designed to end in a more secluded den of vice.

He drank his first glass of champagne in silent praise of the mighty Bras-de-Fer.

His second glass was raised to his lips, and—fell from his trembling hand.

His comrades laughed. They thought it was a slip.

Pale as death, Alphonse asked to be excused for a few moments, and left the table.

Clinton Hastings was waiting for him.

"Ah, my dear brother! I knew I should find you here, and I came at once to reassure you. I was so afraid you might believe that paragraph in the paper, and I knew how sad it would make you."

"What do you want now?"

Alphonse could hardly speak.

"Why, you see that clumsy fellow you sent the money by must have made a mistake, for he only gave me twenty thousand francs. May be he kept the other ten. Anyhow, he didn't give it to me, and I thought you'd be obliged to me if I told you right away."

Alphonse could not tell, from the mockery in Clinton's manner, what had really taken place between him and Bras-de-Fer. He decided to act as if he was innocent of any evil design.

"The villain!" he exclaimed; "I gave him the full amount."

"The wretch! And he only gave me twenty thousand. I'm awfully sorry for you, brother!"

·Sorry for me! Why?"

"Because I must have the other ten thousand to-morrow, and I am afraid it will push you to lend it to me."

"I can't do it. Positively can't."

"Well, of course, if you can't, you can't. I guess D'Iberri will have it, or Grace will, may be, so never mind. *Au revoir.*"

"What time to-morrow will you be at home?"

"All day, dear brother, for your sake. Shall I see you then?"

"Yes."

"Thank you. Good-by. Oh, I say, brother dear, please come yourself. I don't like your messengers."

Alphonse only nodded his head.

Clinton persisted, with a pleasant smile.

"But you will be sure, will you not, dear brother? I feel that I must see you. I cannot let the long days go by without a glimpse now and then of your happy face. Until to-morrow, then, eh?"

"I will bring the money myself to-morrow."

"*Au revoir*, then, dear Alphonse."

Alphonse looked after his tormentor, and said to himself:

"Another check, and a signature this time! How came that ruffian to fail? How came that paragraph in the paper? If I have to do it myself, you mocking devil, it shall be done. Now I must go see that Bras-de-Fer, and learn what happened."

A muffled voice bade him enter, when he knocked at Bras-de-Fer's door.

He found that personage lying on a lounge, his face bandaged, one hand swathed in cloths, and one arm in splints and a sling.

"Ah, monsieur, I have been expecting you. You see me? Well, Bras-de-Fer has found his master. That artist, that American, is the devil."

"And after all your boasting, you failed. And my money?"

Bras-de-Fer looked very sheepish.

"Wait a little. I will succeed next time."

"What have you done with the money?"

"Monsieur, I swear to you that artist shall die."

"But the money you did not earn, where is it?"

"*Au diable* with your money!"

Bras-de-Fer started up in a rage.

"Do you say money to me again and I will tear you with my teeth! What I said I will do I will do. But give me time."

"Vile beast!" muttered Alphonse. Then aloud, soothingly: "Tell me how it happened?"

"Tell you! Yes, I will tell you. I knocked at his door. 'Come in,' said he.

"I went in. He was daubling away on a picture. He did not turn. 'Oh, ho,' said he, and I could see that he saw me in a mirror. 'Are you a brother of my friend? I have met three of his brothers already.'

"'I know nothing about your friend or his brothers,' said I, for I was mad to have him laugh so easy as he was doing.

"'I have come to bring you some money from the man of the black mask.'

"'Oh, ho,' said he, 'my old friend of the window, eh? And you are not his brother?'

"'No, I am not his brother, you laughing devil,' said I.

"'Ho, ho!' he laughed again, and I wanted to choke him.

"'There is your money,' said I, throwing the money on the table, as I told you I would. 'Count it.'

"'Pick up what fell,' said he.

"'Pick it up yourself,' said I.

"'Ho, ho!' he laughed. 'Must I make you pick it up?'

"'Make me? I'll make you!' and with that, I was so mad with his laughing, that I jumped at him with my knife.

"But he caught hold of me like a vise, and laughed in my face.

"I struggled. He took the knife away.

"'I'll give you something to remember me by,' said he and he slit my nose.

"I grabbed the knife and cut my hand. He laughed again.

"Then he threw me away, and said, 'Pick up that money.'

"I said, 'No!'

"He laughed, and broke my arm with a chair.

"'Pick up that money,' said he.

"And I picked it up. But I hate him. I can hear him laugh now; and I tell you, monsieur, when I am well, he dies!"

It was an uneasy night that Alphonse passed. He, too, seemed to continually hear the diabolical laugh of Clinton.

CHAPTER XL.

THE MISTAKE ELISE MADE.

"How are the turtle doves to-day?"

Bras-de-Fer had unceremoniously entered the apartment of Elise, and had caught Tete-de-Fer with his arm about her.

"At least," growled Tete-de-Fer, "you might knock."

"Tush, Robert," said Elise, smiling sweetly at the intruder. "You are too formal. Between friends no ceremony, eh?"

"Quite right, my pretty Elise; but your Robert is such a gentleman that he believes in knocking. He always does it himself. I remember a bank we visited once to study its system—or wasn't it at that bank you knocked so hard? Never mind; it was some bank, and he thought the janitor's head was the door. *Ciel!* how he knocked!"

Bras-de-Fer treated Tete-de-Fer to one of his provoking laughs, and then continued, addressing Elise:

"We are going to bid you good-by, my butterfly!"

"We? Who?"

"Your Robert and I."

"I!" exclaimed Tete-de-Fer. "Where am I going?"

"You are going to D'Iberri after five thousand francs."

"And you, where are you going?"

"That is none of your business, but I will tell you. I am going to London now, but you will hear from me if you do not see me at D'Ibèrri."

"But I do not like going to D'Iberri."

"Elise, do you hear that fellow? He says he does not wish to go and bring away five thousand francs."

Elise curled her lip in scorn, and leaned lazily back on her lounge.

"He wants to live in idleness on my savings," she said.

"It is not so!" exclaimed Tete-de-Fer.

"It is so. I know you."

"Well, I will not go."

Elise shrugged her round shoulders and looked at Bras-de-Fer.

"You hear him. He says he will not go."

Bras-de-Fer laughed.

"He always says that, but he always goes."

"This time I will not go."

Again Bras-de-Fer laughed.

"This time you will do as you always do—you will go. Tell him, Elise, that if he does not go you will leave him."

"You hear?" said Elise, obediently. "Go, or I will leave you."

Tete-de-Fer stared, then scowled and stamped his foot.

"I will not go. It is a trick to get rid of me, *ami*."

Bras-de-Fer did not laugh now; he was grim.

"*Ami*, look at me. So! Do I mean what I say when I tell you 'Go?'"

Tete-de-Fer shuffled his feet, and tried to evade the penetrating gray eyes.

"Answer me!"

"Yes."

"And you say you will not go?"

"But if you stay and Elise stays——"

"Ass! Did I not say I was also going away?"

"But when?"

"Do you question me? You!"

Tete-de-Fer trembled.

"I do not question, but——"

"Did you say you will not go?"

"If I go?"

"If you go? Do you say you will not go?"

"No."

"Ah!"

Bras-de-Fer laughed again now.

"Do you see, Elise, what a fool this Robert of yours is?"

"I have long seen that."

"But do you know what is the matter with him?"

Elise smiled and shook her head.

Tete-de-Fer stood sullenly by devouring his anger and humiliation.

"He is jealous."

And Bras-de-Fer burst into a loud laugh, in which he was joined by Elise.

"Jealous of me! Why, you poor fool, I have not made love to Elise yet. When I do you will have some cause, you may be sure."

"What must I do in D'Iberri?"

"You will go to the mayor and tell him who you are—that is, so far as the marriage at the chateau is concerned."

"And then?"

"Then you will say in that polite way of yours: 'Monsieur the Mayor, one thousand francs, if you please.' He will squirm, but you will insist, and then he will give it to you. But take care—he will tickle you if he can."

"And then?"

"Then you will enjoy yourself quietly in the country for a few days, and go to him again and again, until you have five thousand francs."

"Yes."

"After that wait for me. I shall be near you."

"When must I go?"

"In half an hour. You catch the train then. Now I am off. *Au revoir*, pretty Elise."

Bras-de-Fer went down stairs laughing.

Tete-de-Fer followed him half an hour later cursing.

Half an hour after that there was a knock at the door, and Elise, lying on the lounge with her hands clasped under her head, said:

"Come in."

Clinton Hastings put his head in and smiled diffidently.

"I beg your pardon, mademoiselle, but I thought I heard a man's voice.

"What of it?" she demanded, insolently.

"Nothing, indeed," stammered he; "but I would not otherwise have intruded. I—I beg your pardon."

Elise smiled. This modest young man amused her.

"Don't be in such a hurry. What did you want?"

"It was the time. My clock has stopped. I am sorry to have to trouble you."

Elise smiled again.

"Are you my neighbor, then?"

"The next room, mademoiselle."

"Indeed!"

Elise looked bewitchingly interested.

"Yes, mademoiselle, since yesterday week."

"Do come in, monsieur. There is the clock. I am too lazy to move. Sit down for a moment. What is your occupation?"

"I am an artist, if you please, mademoiselle."

Clinton made a great show of embarrassment, to the extreme delight of the mischievous Elise, who had made up her mind to the amusement of a flirtation.

"An artist! And do you paint portraits?"

"When I can get them to paint."

Elise laughed merrily. This innocent young man pleased her.

"If I were rich, you should paint my portrait."

"If mademoiselle wishes," exclaimed Clinton, eagerly; "money is not necessary. It would be so much happiness to paint such beauty. If you only——"

Clinton stopped in embarrassment.

Elise shook with mirth. The young man was an easy victim.

"Why, monsieur, if you talk like that I shall be proud. When shall we commence?"

"Now, if you will."

"Here?"

"No. In my room. I have better light there."

"Come along."

Elise led the way out.

CHAPTER XLI.

ALPHONSE IS SHOCKED.

"Now," said Clinton, when they were in his studio, "if mademoiselle will say how she will pose, we may begin at once. But first let me mix my paints. Excuse me for a few moments."

Clinton went behind a screen, and Elise employed her time looking at some very hideous daubs scattered about the room. Suddenly she was startled by a voice:

"Hold! What does the pretty tiger-cat here?"

"Bras-de-Fer?"

"At your service, my pretty Elise. *Ciel!* but would not that poor Robert be crazy if he could come home and find you here?"

"But you, Bras-de-Fer, how came you here?"

"How came I here? Why, that is good! Is not this my room?"

"And the artist?"

"What artist?"

"He who came to my room."

"How should I know the artist who came to your room?"

"But he whom I followed here?"

Elise pulled aside the screen, and seeing no one there, stared at Bras-de-Fer.

"Well," said he, "what do you find so strange there?"

"Bras-de-Fer," she said, going up to him and speaking earnestly, "tell me what this means?"

Bras-de-Fer laughed pleasantly. He had gone far enough with the mystification.

"It means that I and the artist are the same."

"The same?"

"Yes; if mademoiselle pleases, I am an artist sometimes."

Bras-de-Fer had taken the manner of the artist.

Elise clapped her hands.

"I shall believe Robert now. You *are* the devil!"

"Poor Robert! Can you guess why I sent him away?"

Elise looked admiringly at him, and did not answer.

"Oh, no," said he, noting the admiration, "not that I am going to rouse the demon of jealousy in his breast, but not on my own account."

Elise flushed.

She felt foolish at having made such a mistake as to suppose he was in love with her.

She was not angry, however.

"Elise, I am going to take you into my confidence."

She looked pleased.

"A man I hate is coming here to-day, to give me some money. I want you to help me to my revenge. Will you?"

"Bras-de-Fer," said Elise, "since the day you conquered me, you have been my master, I think." She held her head down and went on: "I think you never will love me, but I love you. I will do whatever you ask."

He looked at her kindly for a moment and took her hand in his.

"My pretty little Elise, I am very sorry. I never can love you. I already love a woman who has my whole heart. I am very sorry. It is better to be frank with you."

The tiger-cat was no longer visible in Elise. She trembled when he took her hand, and her voice was husky when she spoke.

"It was folly in me to think of it even for a moment. But never mind. I will do—will be happy to do anything you ask. I will do whatever you ask. I will not make you think of this again. I know what you are. You will never change. At least, you respect me?"

"Respect you and admire you, Elise."

"Well, *ami*, what can I do for you?"

"I will give you full instructions."

*   *   *   *   *   *   *

A few hours later, a soft voice bade Alphonse enter.

"I am looking for Monsieur Hastings," said Alphonse, gazing in wonderment at the beautiful creature lying on the lounge.

"Are you?"

Half impudently, half pettishly.

"Does he live here?"

"He says he does."

"Well, doesn't he? May I come in?"

"I don't care."

"But, my little beauty——"

"Don't call me your little beauty."

"How savage you are!"

"Wouldn't anybody be savage?"

She half rose on her elbow in well-feigned excitement.

"Here I've been waiting for him two hours and more. Is he a king or an emperor, that he treats me so? He shall see if I will stand it."

She threw herself back again defiantly.

Alphonse was fascinated by her sensuous beauty.

"Whom have you been waiting for?"

"Whom? Why, Monsieur Hastings. But he will see. Hush!"

She sank back in alarm.

"Here he comes. Don't tell him what I said. I was only joking."

She seemed terribly frightened.

The footstep passed the door and ascended the stairs.

Alphonse wondered at the meaning of this strange scene.

"Why should you fear him? he asked, approaching her.

"Who said I feared him? I don't fear him."

Another footstep made her start, and she waved her hand beseechingly at Alphonse.

"Oh, stand back, stand back. Please don't be so near me. He would "——

She listened.

"It wasn't he. I will go if he doesn't come. I won't wait his pleasure so. I am not his slave if he does——"

She stopped.

"If he does what?" asked Alphonse, in his sweetest tones.

"You are his friend."

"His friend!"

Alphonse laughed bitterly.

"I hate him."

"Do you really?"

Her brown eyes sparkled.

"I do, with all my heart."

She shook her head sadly, and her eyes filled with tears.

"So do I; but he makes me do his will. He makes you do it, too."

She looked at him questioningly.

"Just now; but the time will come."

Alphonse spoke bravely. He was anxious to make the young woman confide in him.

Partly because he was a little in love, and partly because he thought he might learn something useful about Clinton.

"You look like a brave man."

"I can act like one."

"Could you? Could you? but, no, you would not dare."

"Would not dare what? Speak out. Do not be afraid. I would dare anything for such a lovely creature as you."

"Oh, don't say such things. He might come. And if he should hear you he would——"

Again she broke off in a fright.

"Is he so very dreadful, then?" asked Alphonse, nervously.

She listened intently a moment, then sprang to her feet, and threw off a large shawl in which she had been wrapped.

She was in full dress.

She was arrayed exactly as Grace had been the night of her wedding with Clinton.

Alphonse was dazzled by the splendor of her animal beauty.

"You see me?"

She turned around with a sort of fierce disdain.

"Yes; and you are the most beautiful woman I ever did see."

She looked pleased, but pointed hurriedly to one of her plump shoulders.

A black-and-blue spot was plainly visible.

She suddenly stopped, listened, caught up the shawl, and, wrapping herself in it, threw herself on the lounge.

"Stand over there. Don't tell him I took the shawl off."

It was another false alarm.

Alphonse was by this time in a perfect fever of anxiety.

The woman's beauty allured him, and her evident abject fear of Clinton filled him with a nervous dread.

"What does this man?" he asked, when the cause for alarm had passed.

She spoke almost in a whisper.

"You will not betray me to him?"

"Never."

"I would tear you to pieces if you did. It is only he I am afraid of."

Her brown eyes snapped.

It was a new phase of her beauty to see her so fiery.

Alphonse was more than ever fascinated.

"I would not betray you."

"He makes me wear this dress and then curses me fearfully. It makes my blood run cold. I am afraid he will kill me sometimes. And day before yesterday I refused to put it on. Then he struck me."

Elise let her voice fall, and her eyes grew large with horror at the thought of the awful scene.

Alphonse was filled with mingled indignation and terror.

Strike that lovely creature!

But it only showed what a demon the man was.

"Where do you live?" he asked.

"In the next room."

"How can I see you so this devil cannot interrupt us?"

"What do you want to see me for?"

"To help you."

"You can't help me. Nobody can. I ran away from him in America and came here. He was sitting in my room when I awoke one morning."

"Did he beat you?"

"No. Worse."

"What?"

"He laughed."

Alphonse shuddered.

He remembered that laugh.

"Nevertheless I can help you, if you will let me see you. You are not afraid to see me alone?"

"Afraid!"

Elise laughed merrily.

"Of you? Oh, no. I'm only afraid of him."

"Will you see me then?"

"Yes. If he discovers it, he can only kill me. What day is this?"

"Wednesday."

"Thursday morning until noon he is never here. He goes out of the city. Come to-morrow morning at eleven."

"Let me come at ten."

"If you like."

"At nine?"

"Ten will do. Hush!"

The door was thrown open, and Clinton Hastings walked in.

CHAPTER XLII.

IN THE SIREN'S TOILS.

He looked quickly from one to the other; then harshly demanded of her:

"How long has he been here?"

"Five minutes."

She shrank back, as if expecting a blow.

Clinton turned sharply to Alphonse.

"Dear brother, admire and criticise this picture."

Pointing to a landscape on an easel.

"It is that dear old Chateau d'Iberri."

Alphonse bit his lip, and turned to look at it.

"Mademoiselle, go home."

"Yes, monsieur," was the meek answer.

Alphonse turned to look at her; but Clinton adroitly screened her, and went on in his mocking way:

"The dear old Chateau! What happy memories it recalls, does it not, dear brother?"

"I have brought your money."

"That is a good brother."

"Will you leave me in peace now?"

"In peace, dear brother? Can you ask?"

"Yes, I can and do ask. If you are going to persecute me and bleed me as you have done, I might as well let you go to D'Iberri at once."

"And how sad that would be!"

"Mock me if you will, but I tell you, you have done your worst already. I refuse to give you anything more."

Alphonse was trying Clinton.

Clinton seemed to hesitate.

"What! not even to keep me from going to D'Iberri?"

Alphonse felt that he was gaining a triumph.

"Not even for that. My money is exhausted, and I can get no more. So you see it will be useless to urge me any further."

"But D'Iberri still has plenty, and Grace can perhaps get it for me. You are right; it is unfair to ask you for any more. The next time I will go to Grace. Good-by."

Clinton laughed, and Alphonse saw that he had merely been mocking him.

"Tell me, then, what I am to expect from you?"

"I couldn't do it, dear brother. I want to keep you in suspense. I want you to feel that when I crook my finger you must come. I want you to feel that six thousand dollars a year depend upon my silence. I want you to feel that I can put you in prison for that altered check or that forged check. I want you to feel that I can hang you for that murder in America."

All this was said in a light tone of mockery, but it none the less chilled Alphonse to the very marrow. He saw that his every movement was known to this man.

It was not a mere persecution he was suffering—it was a life and death struggle he was engaged in.

The very desperation of the case gave him presence of mind to act.

"I am in your power. I will do as you require."

Again that hateful laugh.

"You are wise. You may go now."

The next day at ten o'clock found Alphonse in Elise's room.

She was dressed in a charming *neglige*, and, reclining in an easy-chair, was sipping a cup of chocolate.

All the fear of the former day was gone, and she was seductively languid and vivacious by turns.

Alphonse was divided between his fast increasing passion for her and his desire to rid himself of Clinton.

"Well, *ami*," she said, "you went away conquered yesterday, eh?"

"Why do you think that?"

"Oh!"—a pretty shrug of the shoulders—"I listened. And then he was so good-natured after you were gone."

"And you heard all he said to me?"

"Yes," indifferently. "Forgery, murder and all."

Alphonse ground his teeth.

"And you believed him?"

"Why not? He made you do those things, very likely. Oh, as he often says himself, he is the devil, I think."

"I will kill him."

"No, you will not."

"Why?"

"You cannot. Only a few days ago he said to me, 'Elise, get behind that screen and you will see some fun. A man is coming here to murder me.'

"I pretended to be alarmed for him. He laughed at me —that laugh of his which seems to say 'I know your real thoughts.'

"Then he said, 'My pretty Elise, the fun will be your disappointment when the man fails.'

"*Mon Dieu*! He was right. I would give my teeth, one by one"—she showed her gleaming white teeth—"to have him dead.

"But see how it happened. The man came. A perfect Hercules of a fellow. Monsieur mocked him and gibed him till he was crazy.

"Then he pulled a big knife and jumped at him.

"*Grand Dieu*! I thought I was free.

"No, monsieur only laughed and—ah! it was frightful how he punished the poor fellow.

"Then he said to me, 'I will put a paragraph in the papers saying I am dead. My dear brother will read it and be happy for a day. You, too, may read it, and perhaps it will make you feel good for a moment.'"

"What a monster! exclaimed Alphonse.

"Yes, indeed. Oh, he cannot be killed! When he first met me I was fierce. I thought no man could master me. He did it by laughing at me, and I hated him. I said I would kill him.

"One day he was asleep on the lounge, and I took my dagger—I always carry it now, he makes me. I have to show it to him every day, and then he laughs. Ah! how I hate him.

"Well, this day I crept up softly, intending just to stratch his face—there is deadly poison on the point. It was only an inch from his cheek, when he had my wrist in his hand, and he was laughing.

"Kill him! no. He is the devil."

Elise had told these stories with all the animation of an exasperated woman, and then had sunk despairingly back in her chair.

Alphonse was deeply impressed.

The mysterious confidence and extraordinary power and knowledge of Clinton augmented his fear, but only made him the more anxious to put his enemy out of the way.

He knew he was only being saved for a purpose, and that either he must kill Clinton or look forward to some terrible punishment, all the more to be dreaded that it was hidden in mystery.

He saw that he had been entangling himself in a mesh of Clinton's weaving, and he swore to himself that he would accomplish his enemy's destruction.

Not one thought of Grace entered his selfish mind, although he must have known that she, too, would some time be a victim.

"Well," said Elise, after Alphonse had remained silent several minutes, "will you kill him?"

"Suppose I were to hire two men to do it?"

"Ten men would be like children to him."

"Wait! I have it! Do the people of the house know that you and he are acquainted?"

"No. He was furious when he saw you in the studio with me. I could see it in his eyes. I thought he would strike me. Nobody knows."

"Then, if he should die of poison, nobody would suspect you?"

"No. But he won't die of poison."

"Why?"

"Who will give it to him?"

"I will."

"How can you?"

"Tell me his habits. Does he drink chocolate?"

"No; coffee. I prepare it for him every morning."

"Then I will be here some morning and put arsenic in his coffee."

"And I will carry it to him?"

"Yes."

"No, monsieur. He would look into my eyes and read poison there."

"But think, Elise, what a deliverance if we could get him out of the way!"

"Yes."

Elise sighed and looked pensive.

"But I could never stand his eyes on me."

"You are not in earnest, Elise."

"In earnest!"

She started from her chair.

"I would give anything to see him dead!"

"Would you give——"

Alphonse gazed on her passionately, and caught her hand in his.

"Would you give your love?"

A quick change from excitement to coquetry passed over the sensuous face.

"I might try."

Alphonse fervently kissed her dimpled hand and moved to put his arm around her waist.

She glided away from him, and exclaimed, with an arch laugh:

"He is still alive."

Alphonse bit his lip. The love was evidently very much one-sided.

However, he would gain her and kill Clinton yet, he promised himself.

"Can you suggest any way?"

"He drinks a small glass of brandy every night before going to bed."

"Yes."

"And his bottle is easy to get."

"I will put arsenic in it."

"Arsenic! Bah! He would tell it in a moment. As if that were the only poison."

"What then?"

"See!"

She stooped and drew from the under side of the lounge a small vial of colorless liquid.

"That paralyzes the throat and kills in agony in half an hour. I have had it a month, and have not dared to use it."

Her brown eyes snapped as she went on:

"He has kept me like a whipped dog, and I wish to look at him when he dies and enjoy his agony. If he drinks this, he cannot speak to call for help, and I can taunt him till he dies."

Alphonse eagerly took the vial.

"When can I put it in the brandy?"

"Not now. Oh, he would discover it somehow! He will be home at noon. He will stay home till six, and go out for dinner, and return at nine to go to bed. That is the usual way. After he goes out at six he seldom wants to see me again. Then you may come and fix the brandy, and I need not betray the trap."

"I will be here."

Alphonse rubbed his hands gleefully. He felt assured of success.

"And then you will love me?"

"Oh! I only said I would try."

"But you *will* try?"

"I guess so."

"Try a little now."

"What's the use?"

"Just to encourage me."

"Well, I will, then."

"Beautiful Elise, may I kiss you?"

"Yes."

Alphonse sprang eagerly forward to press her lips.

"My hand, I mean."

She laughed at his discomfiture as she retreated behind a chair and held out her hand.

He quickly recovered himself.

"Your hand is better than any other woman's lips."

And he devoured the plump little fingers with warm kisses.

Alphonse was infatuated. He was in the toils of the siren.

CHAPTER XLIII.

THE TRIUMPH OF ALPHONSE.

"Has he gone?"

"Yes, and will be back soon. He is very tired. Quick!"

Elise thrust the vial into Alphonse's hand, and let him into the studio by a door opening from her room.

A dim light burning, showed a half-bottle of brandy and a small glass standing on a little table by the bedside.

"Shall I put it into the brandy?" whispered he.

"Yes."

"Is there enough here to kill?"

"Half of it would do. Quick! I am dying of fright."

The vial was emptied into the brandy.

The liquor became clouded and then cleared again.

"Now come in here," she whispered, and closed the door securely.

"Where shall I wait?" he asked.

"Oh, you must not leave me, or I shall die."

"Why not fly with me?"

"He might want me when he returns. If I were not here he would suspect."

"What of it? We would be safe."

"He would find us. Besides, I want to see his agony."

"Where shall I hide, then?"

"In the closet. And see, there is a little hole through the partition. You can watch him. When you see the poison take effect call me. He cannot cry out. He cannot live."

The dim light in Elise's apartment; the low whispers; the woman's chattering teeth, were not calculated to encourage Alphonse.

He was in a clammy perspiration, and a nervous dread overcame him.

What if Clinton, with his mysterious knowledge of everything, should suspect?

"Perhaps I had better wait outside in the street," he said.

"And leave me here alone? No. You shall stay here."

Elise spoke fiercely.

Alphonse crept into the closet and glued his eyes to the hole.

He could see everything distinctly.

A half-hour dragged slowly along. Alphonse fifty times wished himself away.

He would have gone, but love for the woman, and fear and hate for the man held him back.

At last Clinton came in.

He turned up the lamp and sat down. Alphonse could see every movement.

Clinton sat brooding, angrily.

Suddenly he looked fixedly at the door of Elise's room, and stepped lightly toward it.

Alphonse could not see him now, but his heart beat violently.

Could he suspect?

Clinton rapped sharply on the door.

"Elise!"

"Oh, *mon Dieu!*" she exclaimed, with a stifled shriek. "He has discovered; he will kill me. Yes, monsieur."

She tried to steady her voice.

Alphonse suffered agonies. If Clinton discovered him he would kill him like a rat in a trap.

"Open the door."

"Yes, monsieur."

The door was opened.

"What did you go into the studio for, eh? Answer or I will choke you."

"I did not, monsieur. I swear I did not."

"This door has been opened. Quick! The truth."

"I—I opened the door because my dress was caught."

"That's a lie; but never mind. I will find out if you do not tell me, and then so much the worse for you, my serpent, my tiger-cat!"

"It is the truth, monsieur."

She was sobbing.

Clinton closed the door. Alphonse breathed again.

The artist threw off his coat and boots, and, rolling a cigarette, lighted it and lay down on the bed.

He rose, leaned on his elbow, and took up the bottle of brandy.

Alphonse felt his knees knocking each other.

Clinton paused as he was about to pour out the liquor, and held the bottle up to the light.

Alphonse shook as with palsy, and would have given up all thoughts of vengeance to have been safely in the street.

He did not dare to move.

The inspection seemed to satisfy Clinton, for he poured the brandy into the glass.

Then his suspicions seemed to revive, for he smelled of the brandy.

He looked toward the door as if half-minded to call Elise.

The glass was almost at his lips, when he withdrew it and examined it by the lamp-light.

Every hesitating movement caused Alphonse an angony of fear.

At last Clinton frowned, tossed his head, and drank down the brandy.

Beads of cold perspiration stood on the forehead of Alphonse as with staring eyes he watched Clinton.

Five minutes passed, and still the artist puffed away calmly.

Suddenly he stiffened his body and threw away his cigarette.

He half rose in bed and fell again, clutching at his throat and making a gurgling noise.

His body bent like a bow. His features were contorted as if the musles were tying themselves into knots.

The clutching at the throat and gurgling went on.

Alphonse turned sick at his stomach and rushed from the closet.

Elise was on her knees with her hands clasped, her face full of terror.

"He is dying," hoarsely whispered Alphonse. "Come, let us fly."

"He took it?"

Elise sprang to her feet eagerly.

Alphonse nodded.

"Then let us go in, that he may know who did it. Oh, I can love you for this. Come."

"No, no—for Heaven's sake, no! It is awful."

"Bah! Come, I say."

She turned on him fiercely.

"Are you afraid of a dying man? Come, I say."

She dragged him after her to the door, eagerly threw it open, and led him in.

Clinton was undergoing fearful agonies, as his writhing body and convulsed features proved.

His speechless suffering was terrible.

Elise laughed like a madwoman.

"Aha!" she hissed, as Clinton's glaring eyes fell upon her. "You will choke me, eh? You will beat me, eh? You will curse me, eh? I am a snake, eh? See, here is the man who did it! And I am to love him for it. I am to love him—do you hear, love him? Ha, ha! you suffer, do you? You cannot speak, you cannot laugh any more!"

She went up close to him, and shook her little fist in his face with the air of a fury.

"Shall I put a paragraph in the papers for this dear brother to read, eh?"

Clinton made one supreme effort to rise, and then fell back stiff.

"Now come," said Elise, coolly, to Alphonse.

And she led him fainting from the room, and closed the door.

"Let us go away from here," he gasped.

"Us? No, indeed. *You* must go, but *I* must stay. If I were to go I would be suspected. Now go quickly, or you will be suspected."

"Ah! I thought you would go with me."

"What folly! Go, and do not come back for a week, or you may get in trouble."

"Not see you for a whole week?"

"What is a week? We are both young. Will you go?"

"At least you will kiss me now?"

"I have not learned to love you yet. I am only trying now."

Elise laughed gayly.

Alphonse thought of the dead man in the next room, and shuddered.

"Are you not afraid to stay here alone with—with him in the next room?"

Elise laughed until she cried.

"Oh, what a joke! Afraid of a dead man! No, indeed, nor of any living one now. Good-night, monsieur, good-night."

And Elise pushed him out of her room.

"But," he pleaded, "I may see you in a week."

"Yes."

The door was shut and bolted.

Alphonse crept in horror past the artist's door, and flew down the stairs.

His footsteps had hardly ceased to sound on the stairs when Elise put her head into the studio and burst into a peal of laughter.

Clinton sat up and smiled quietly and approvingly.

"Now you are companions in crime," he said.

"Yes."

And again Elise laughed.

"Oh, *mon Dieu!* But he was frightened when he saw you twist and turn. I thought he would faint. Oh, but you did it beautifully."

"What I did was nothing, Elise, but you—you are a perfect actress. Do you think he is much in love?"

"Head and ears. He is crazy with love. How I will tease him, the cowardly little puppy! And he shall forge a check for ten thousand francs every week. Love him, indeed!"

"You are doing a great deal for me, Elise."

"You know I am glad?"

She flushed, and her lip trembled.

"Yes, Elise, I know it, and I am grateful. I wish I could repay you."

"If you are satisfied with me, it is enough."

He took her hand and kissed it respectfully.

The warm blood rushed to her face, and she tottered as if about to fall.

He caught her in his arms.

Her soft brown eyes swimming in tenderness looked up at him. The lithe, pliant form was swelling with warm life.

He was a man.

He kissed her.

The next moment he regretted it.

"Oh, Elise, what have I done? It was wrong, wrong."

He placed her in a chair and walked up and down.

"It was my fault," she murmured. "Don't be sorry. It pays me for all I have done, or will do, for you. I will not try to make you do it again."

Clinton smiled.

"You little witch!" he exclaimed. "You conquered me. Well, I forgive you. What a life you will lead that poor Alphonse."

"How I love you!"

She spoke passionately.

Clinton smiled and shook his head.

"I must get away, or there'll be more kisses to regret. Good-night."

"Good-night."

She listened till she could hear his footsteps no more.

"He'll never love me. I know it. But at least he kissed me."

CHAPTER XLIV.

FROM PARIS TO D'IBERRI.

"And we are really going to D'Iberri at last, Honore?"

"Yes, my darling, to dear old D'Iberri. How I long to have you see the old chateau. I hope you will like it. Now that we have started, and are actually on our way there, I have misgivings lest it should be too old and musty for my bright and joyous Grace."

"Honore, I will not talk to you about that. You will see when I am there whether it suits me or not."

Grace looked up at her husband with an air of adoration.

"I am so glad to get away from Paris."

"And I, too. I was so busy all the time that I seemed hardly to see you at all."

"I was very lonesome sometimes."

"Dear little Grace! Well, you shall have me at D'Iberri until you will be glad of a respite."

"You don't believe that, Honore, do you?"

"I should be sorry if I did, for it would make me very unhappy if I thought you could tire of me for even a minute."

"We shall be so happy there, Honore."

"Indeed we shall."

"I am glad Alphonse refused to come with us."

"So am I, and yet——"

Honore frowned.

"What, darling?"

"I did not like to leave him behind. He is so dissipated. More so, it seems to me, than ever. And I don't know Grace—it is foolish of me, of course—but I have a strange feeling of uneasiness about him."

"Don't think of him, Honore. He worries me, too; but I know he will not change for anything we could say, so let us be happy—just as happy as two children in vacation time."

"So we will, my Grace."

"No more ceremony, no more fashions to keep up. Only

simple me and simple—no, that won't do. I can't call you simple. You, my dignified and noble husband," she laughed. "But just 'us—our two selves. Oh, but shall we not be happy?"

Honore smiled lovingly at his vivacious wife.

"Tell me what D'Iberri is like, so I can see it from far away. How near does the cars take us?"

"Five miles. At D'Iberri, the little town, the carriage will be waiting for us, and we will reach the chateau at sunset. It stands on a little plateau, and I want you to tell me if you ever saw anything more beautiful. I timed it to reach there at sunset on purpose that you might enjoy it."

"How thoughtful of you."

"Then we will have supper at once. After that, if you are not too tired, I will show you the chateau interior by candle-light."

Grace clapped her hands with the enthusiasm of a child.

"You shall have a few lamps in the chateau," went on Honore, smiling; "but there are such beautiful bronze and silver candelabras that I can't bear not to use them; besides, the effect when they are all lighted is splendid."

"It must be. Don't apologize. Am I not going to be a real country housekeeper?"

"And then they are so much more in keeping with the antique furniture."

"I am so glad you did not send it away, Honore. It gives you so much pleasure."

"So it does. It would have been a positive sacrifice to have replaced it by new furniture. But I would not have hesitated if you had wished me to change it."

"I know it, you dear husband; but I would not have it changed for anything."

"I have given orders to have the whole chateau lighted while we are at supper, so that you may see the inside as well as the outside at its best. You see I am a schemer."

"A dear old schemer."

Lovers never find the time long, and Grace was astonished when Honore told her they were at D'Iberri.

A pretty little phaeton, drawn by two fleet, gray ponies, was waiting for them.

Without neglecting the ponies, Honore kept his eye constantly on Grace.

She was in raptures with the beautiful country.

"I had no idea," she exclaimed, that old Brittany had so many lovely spots. Oh! look at that chateau. Is that D'Iberri?"

Honore smiled, and nodded assent.

"How lovely! Oh! Honore, I shall be happy there. You were right, it is beautiful."

A shade passed over his face.

"Can all this enthusiasm be real?" he asked himself, "or is she a better actress than I supposed. Lovely little demon, I will startle you before this night is over, or I mistake my power."

They drew nearer and nearer to the chateau, and yet, closely as he watched her he could see no sign of recognition in her face.

She was full of joyous enthusiasm.

The gates were opened by old Pierre, all smiles and reverences.

"What a quaint old porter!" exclaimed Grace.

"An old servitor. I could not have the heart to send him away."

"I am so glad you did not."

"Perhaps he will amuse you. He is full of odd stories about the chateau, its ghosts, and the like."

"Has it ghosts?"

Grace made a pretty pretense of alarm.

"Not very dangerous ones, I guess," laughed Honore.

"Ah! what lovely marble steps!" she exclaimed, when she alighted from the phaeton, "and what mosaics."

Honore looked at her and marveled.

They passed through the door and into the hall, and on every hand Grace saw some new object to admire.

"I do not understand this; but it is real," said Honore to himself. "Either she has forgotten, or she never saw this part of the chateau before. After supper we shall see, my child-like little wife, my lovely Grace, my demon."

CHAPTER XLV.

THE CHATEAU BY CANDLE-LIGHT.

"Now show me my future home," exclaimed Grace, when the meal was over.

"We will go into the great saloon first."

Honore led the way up the broad staircase and stopped in front of the double doors of the saloon.

"Now," said he, smiling, "prepare for a burst of splendor."

He threw the doors open and led Grace in.

An exclamation of pleasure broke from her lips, and ended in a quick gasp as her eyes took in the detail of the room, and memory woke within her.

She cast a quick glance of terror on her husband.

He was smiling happily.

She clung to his arm and shut her eyes.

"Do you like it, Grace?"

The blue eyes opened and stared wildly around. They closed and opened again.

The little hands frantically felt of the strong arm they clung to.

"Is this you, Honore?" she panted.

"Yes, darling. What is the matter? Are you ill?

"Are we in—in—D'Iberri?

"Yes, my darling. Grace, dear, what is it?"

"I—I—don't know. I—I—think—I—oh! Honore, take me away—take me away!"

She threw herself into his arms and clung there sobbing and trembling.

"Oh! my darling, what is the matter?"

He lifted her tenderly and carried her into an adjoining room to place her on a lounge.

She opened her eyes and glanced despairingly around.

They were in the square chamber.

A scream burst from her lips, and breaking from her husband's arms she ran shrieking from the room.

He was by her side in a moment, and once more taking her in his arms carried her into their own room, where he laid her gently on the bed, and tried to soothe her.

She clung to him, repeating incoherently over and over again:

"You will not leave me, will you?"

"No, darling; no, I am not going to leave you," he would answer.

But nothing seemed to reassure her. She would not cease to cling wildly to him, now whispering to herself, and now imploring him frantically not to leave her.

To all his questions she would make no answer, only shaking her head and sobbing.

At last she became more 'calm, and finally closed her eyes and slept.

Her husband lay by her side, and ere long he, too, was breathing regularly.

By this time it was midnight, and all the servants had retired to rest.

Presently Grace partially rose in bed and listened to Honore's regular breathing.

Then she silently slipped out of bed and stole noiselessly from the room, closing the door after her.

The moment she did so, her husband rose from the bed and pressed his thumb against the wall.

A panel moved out of place.

Honore passed through the opening and disappeared. The panel slid back to its proper position.

Grace sped swiftly and silently across the hall and entered the square chamber.

She pressed her two hands over her mouth and stifled a cry that rose to her lips.

There was a hunted look in her eyes as she stared around her.

"Yes," she murmured, with blanched lips; "this is the room."

She walked wildly to the middle of the chamber.

"And this is the very spot."

With a moan upon her lips, she sank upon her knees and clasped her hands.

"Have mercy, oh, Heaven, have mercy! I was so young then; and I meant no harm."

"There is no mercy for such as you!"

The words fell clear and distinct upon her affrighted ear.

She staggered to her feet.

"Who spoke?"

No answer.

"Am I so guilty, then?"

Her reason was slipping from her.

"Yes."

She clasped her hands and looked beseechingly up, as if appealing to Heaven, and then sank limp and lifeless to the floor.

But for that pitiful figure prostrate on the floor, the square chamber, with its scores of flaring candles, might have been mistaken for the same room at midnight not many years before.

A few moments of dead silence, and a panel in one end of the chamber slid noiselessly aside, and Honore stepped forth.

Advancing sternly to the form of his wife, he gazed down at her with a strange mingling of yearning tenderness and bitter scorn.

"This is the beginning of your suffering."

But even as he spoke, his heart gave way, and he knelt beside her.

"How can it be? how can it be? She is outwardly so sweet, so gentle, so loving.

"If I did not know—if I had not the testimony of her own lips and my own senses, I could not believe.

"Oh, my Grace, how I love you!—love you in spite of all my knowledge of your wickedness.

"Why, then, may I not cease my persecution of you, and give myself up to the love that devours me?

"I suffer as much in the infliction as you in the receiving."

He buried his face in his hands.

"No!" he exclaimed, suddenly starting to his feet. "It is this very weakness I must fight.

"Was it not on this very spot that she overwhelmed me with her caresses and at the same time plotted my assassination?

"No. The Marquis d'Iberri may satisfy his love; Clinton Hastings must gratify his hate."

He took her in his arms with infinite tenderness and carried her back to her bed.

CHAPTER XLVI.

OLD PIERRE AMUSES GRACE.

It was only youth and a strong constitution that carried Grace safely through the days of agony which followed the terrible events of that night.

At times it seemed to her that she could not retain her reason.

She would have begged her husband to take her away from the fateful chateau; but every time she thought of such a thing she recalled all that she had promised about remaining there.

And then she would shudder at the thought of passing a whole year or so near those dreadful rooms.

"Why did I not tell him?" she moaned, again and again.

Was it too late now?

Alas! her husband, with terrible foresight, had provided against every emergency.

She could not forget his passion at the mere suggestion that she could ever have loved or caressed another.

It seemed to her that fate was pursuing her for the mistake of her youth.

She ought to have been brave in spite of Honore's words of passion.

She ought to have told him of the secret marriage before she became his wife.

Then she might have died had he thrown her from him.

But now, to have him scorn her for her deception—to have him turn from her.

No, no, she could not bear it.

Better to accept the punishment that came to her than to risk the loss of that beloved husband's love and respect.

And that voice in the square chamber!

Was it a voice, or was it only her disturbed imagination?

She decided that it was her imagination, but yet could not shake off the awful feeling with which it had filled her.

The struggle to keep her trouble from Honore was not the least of her woes.

Loving him so entirely she felt that, in keeping a secret from him, she was every day thrusting him away from her.

When she did not walk about with him, holding fast by his arm, she would follow him with her wistful eyes.

He knew the agony she was suffering, but ascribed it to a guilty and fearful conscience.

How could he so misjudge that gentle creature?

Alas! what man, controlled by his passions, can judge fairly of anything that wounds his egotism.

He, too, suffered; suffered bitterly, and yet he persisted.

He had caused the arbor, where he had been led that fatal night, to be put in order.

And there, when Grace seemed strong enough, he led her.

It was out of the hateful chateau, and she grew to like it there.

One day Honore left her, in order to make a necessary visit to the town.

She took some fancy work and a book, and repaired to the arbor.

As she sat there, old Pierre, who was working near by, looked up, and seeing that she noticed him, took off his old cap in respectful salutation to his lovely young mistress.

Grace recalled what her husband had said of old Pierre's fund of anecdotes, and, with the design of amusing herself, called him to her.

"Why are you at work in the garden?" she asked. "I thought you were our gate porter?"

"So I am, your ladyship; but when his lordship went away he said he'd feel easier if I'd come hereabout and work, in case your ladyship might be lonesome."

"Dear Honore! How good he is," she murmured.

"Well, I am little lonesome, good Pierre," she said, aloud, "and my husband says you know many a legend and story about the old chateau."

"So I do, so I do, your ladyship," answered the delighted old man.

"Come, then, sit down, and tell me one to while away the time."

"Nay, I can stand, your ladyship."

"Not so, good Pierre. Sit, or I will not listen to you."

"Nay, then, if your ladyship insists."

And the old man respectfully sat upon the very edge of his rustic seat.

"What sort of a story are you going to tell me, Pierre?"

"It is for you to say, my lady, for I have all sorts, ghosts and murders and——"

"Oh, gracious! Pierre stop. Why, what dreadful people your D'Iberris must me!"

AND THERE, WHEN GRACE SEEMED STRONG ENOUGH, HE LED HER.

"Nay, your ladyship," said the old man, rather indignantly, "the D'Iberris don't blush before the best in the land."

"Why, I'll not say a word against them, Pierre. But when you speak of ghosts and murders, what must I think? Good folks don't walk the earth when they are dead, and as for murders, why, surely you will not say they are right?"

The old man's care for the honor of the family pleased Grace even while she was amused by it.

Pierre grumbled and shook his head when Grace ceased speaking, for her logic was unanswerable. He was not to be put down, however.

"What your ladyship says is true enough, but I did not say the murders were done by D'Iberris. Why, two murders were done here in this very arbor, and no D'Iberri had a hand in it."

"How was that now?"

Grace settled herself for the story.

"Why, it's not much of a tale, for the most anybody knows is that they were lying dead here one morning."

"And is that all?"

"Mostly all. It was supposed they had killed each other. Oh, the arbor was a sight, I can tell you! They must have struggled terribly.

"Why, right there where you sit is a big spatter of blood, where one of them struck his head."

Grace hurriedly shifted her seat, and looked with curious horror at an irregular dull brown spot on the bench.

"And has this remained all these years?"

"Why, your ladyship, it was not so many years ago. Let me see—it was the fall of '65, I think. I can always remember it by the wax candles I used all that winter."

"How was that?"

Grace was ghastly pale.

"Why, you see I was permitted to let strangers see the chateau in those days; for the present marquis, your husband, had not then come into his title, and the chateau was empty.

"Well, that night, for some odd whim, some strangers had hired the chateau and lit it up with wax candles."

"What month was this?"

"I won't say exactly, but I think November. However, it was the morning after that that the two men were found dead in here."

Grace was on the point of fainting.

"What did the men look like?" she gasped.

Old Pierre was quite unconscious of her agitation.

"As I remember now, one was short and dark and the other was tall and fairish like."

"Did he have a brown beard?"

" Did who have a brown beard?"

" The tall man."

" Now I forget precisely, but since you speak of it, I think he did."

" And gray eyes?"

Pierre was respectfully surprised.

" He might, your ladyship, but I didn't take much notice of it. It was the tall fellow's blood that stained the seat."

" Oh!" Grace sprang to her feet. " And I sat on it! Oh, oh! I shall die here!"

She fled swiftly from the arbor, scarcely conscious of what she was doing.

" Oh!" she groaned, " must I live here amid all these frightful witnesses? May I have no more peace or happiness? Honore, my husband, if you only knew how I suffer!"

CHAPTER XLVII.

PUTTING ON THE SCREWS.

While Grace was undergoing the torture of old Pierre's story, two men were conversing together near an old bridge near the town of D'Iberri.

The larger of the two men had called out to the smaller as he was passing along toward the town:

" Hold, *ami* Tete-de-Fer!"

" Bras-de-Fer!"

" Why, for once, you seem really glad to see me."

" Am I not always glad?"

" I think not. If you held my life in your hands I should not care to see you; but then you are such a kindhearted, forgiving creature, perhaps you are glad to see me."

" How is Elise?"

" I cannot tell. Elise is not my sister. How much money have you received?"

" Three thousand francs. I am to meet the mayor here to-night to receive another thousand."

" Do you always meet here?"

" This will be the first time."

"Has he tried yet to tickle you?"

"No."

"He will to-night."

"How do you know?"

"How do I know anything?"

That was precisely what Tete-de-Fer would have been glad to know.

"He gives up his money very hard."

"What! He grumbles over a few thousand francs? The old miser! he has one hundred thousand in that strong box of his in his room."

"One hundred thousand! Why not make him give up more?"

"You may if you wish. All you get you may have."

Tete-de-Fer's eyes sparkled. He thought how splendid he would make Elise if he had so much money.

"It is like pulling teeth to get money from him."

"Yes, he loves money."

"If I might visit him at his house?"

"You may."

"What! And bring away the strong box?"

"Yes."

"And may I keep all the money?"

"Every sou."

"You are good to me."

"You are a fool. I am not good to you. I am using you."

"When may I do it?"

"When you please."

"Then I will do it to-night."

"If he does not tickle you."

"I will look out for that."

"Will you take some advice?"

"Yes."

"Then, when the mayor comes here, gag him and tie him the first thing. Take the money from him and let him go."

"Why?"

"He is very quick and will stick you. Remember, I warned you once before."

"Good! I will do as you say."

"I do not say—I suggest."

"And after that I may return to Paris?"

"No; you will stay here. You will take this paper and read it. It will tell you just what you are to do. Do exactly as it says, and you may afterward go to Paris."

"But I may be suspected here."

"Not if you do as the paper says."

"Is that all?"

"No. Take this knife and use it to open the strong box with. When that is done, take this piece of paper and pin it to the table with the knife."

"Then you expected me to open the strong box?"

Tete-de-Fer was stupefied.

Bras-de-Fer shrugged his shoulders.

That evening when the mayor met Tete-de-Fer, the latter warily watched for a chance to take the former off his guard.

The former watched the latter in the same way.

The difference was that Tete-de-Fer knew he was watched, while the mayor was quite unconscious that he was suspected.

The mayor entered into conversation.

"I do not like coming out so late at night."

"Bah! what difference does it make?"

"If my wife should know it, I would be accused of all sorts of things."

"Will she not know when you go to bed?"

"No, for I sleep in my own room."

"Are you afraid she will hear the latch-key? You carry the latch-key, I suppose?"

Tete-de-Fer asked this very carelessly, but he waited eagerly for the reply.

"Yes, but I do not use it. I know a trick worth two of that. I have a ladder hidden under the wall, and I get into my window by it."

"You old rascal, you are used to being out late."

"He, he!" giggled the mayor.

"Your window, then, must be at the back of the house?"

"It is. But now let us see about this money. Will five hundred do?"

"One thousand. Nothing less."

"Well, here it is, then."

He was holding the haft of his knife in a firmer grasp when Tete-de-Fer knocked him over the head with a club.

It was his way of saving trouble.

The mayor dropped like a log.

Tete-de-Fer bound and gagged him without stopping to discover if his man might not be dead.

It made very little difference to him, since Bras-de-Fer had not said he must not kill him.

The mayor was not dead, however.

He was found and freed the next morning by some passing peasants.

His story of being afraid of his wife was a little piece of fiction. She was afraid of him.

Nevertheless he would have been glad to have slipped quietly into the house with his bruised and bloody head.

To his dismay, however, the whole house was alive and in an uproar.

They had first missed the mayor, and had noticed a ladder at his window.

It took him just fifteen minutes to silence their clamor over his strange appearance, and to learn that a ladder was at his window.

"My money!" he yelled.

It was his only thought.

He flew up stairs and hurled himself against the door.

The key had been taken from his pocket.

He was a little man, and the door was strong.

He nearly went crazy while he waited for somebody to come with an ax and break the door down.

Suddenly he bethought him of the ladder, and without a word of warning plunged into the terrified crowd behind him, and knocking them right and left, flew down stairs.

Thinking he had become crazy in real earnest they followed him, screeching and crying.

He rushed to the ladder, mounted it, and darted head-foremost through the window.

The strong box was open.

With a howl he sprang to it and peered in.

It was empty.

A knife sticking in the table caught his eye.

The knife pierced a piece of paper, on which was written:

"In memory of November 13, 18——. One good turn deserves another."

When the servants put their heads through the window the mayor was counting imaginary bank-books.

When they entered the room he offered them the empty
box to help themselves from.

He had become generous—and a maniac.

'CHAPTER XLVIII.

A RELIC.

As the days passed on and nothing new occurred to remind Grace of the past, she began to recover something of
her natural serenity.

If Honore noticed that she carefully avoided certain parts
of the house, he said nothing; and, indeed, seemed quite
unconscious that his wife was in any way troubled.

It was a relief to Grace that she was not questioned concerning her pallor and nervousness.

Had she been, she felt that she would have broken down
and confessed all.

And the contemplation of the effect of such a confession
almost drove her frantic.

She knew she had done wrong, but since she was now
doubly assured that Clinton Hastings was dead, she felt
that, in time, she might even come to enter the dreaded
rooms.

If it were possible, she was determined to be happy at
D'Iberri.

She believed it to be a part of her punishment that she
had been brought to pass her life on the scene of the one
mistake of her life.

Like a brave and true-hearted woman, she meekly
accepted her punishment.

The wrong she did her husband in keeping a secret from
him she would endeavor to make up by greater devotion to
his happiness.

With this resolution she gained additional composure.
And if she was less gay and joyous, she was even more gentle
and loving than before, if that were possible.

The color returned to her cheeks, and she began to take
the greatest delight in the work of laying out the grounds
as the warm days of spring had fairly set in.

Her husband entered into the work with the same ardor

as herself.   Indeed it was he who had suggested it as a pleasant pastime.

Together they roamed about the grounds, giving directions and occasionally putting in a plant themselves.

One morning, when they had been occupied thus for some time, Honore proposed going to the arbor to rest.

" No, no!" exclaimed Grace, in alarm.

She had not been able yet to conquer her repugnance to the spot stained by the blood of her first husband.

TOGETHER THEY ROAMED ABOUT THE GROUNDS, GIVING DIRECTIONS AND OCCASIONALLY PUTTING IN A PLANT THEMSELVES.

" But I am afraid you are tired, Grace."

" Indeed I am not Honore.   See, there is that new man who came here two weeks ago; he seems to be looking at something."

" Looking at his hands, I guess, to see if his hard work has blistered them."

Grace laughed, for the new gardener's assistant was notoriously the laziest and poorest workman they had.

"Let us go and see what it is, anyhow."

"As you please, my Grace. The man will be glad of an excuse for talking."

"Why do you keep him, Honore? You are always making fun of his idleness."

"Well, you know, he was recommended to me by that poor Mayor of D'Iberri who has gone crazy, and I don't like to send him away."

"What a soft-hearted fellow you are, Honore!"

"Oh, I can be positively cruel."

"I don't believe it; but here is the man. What is he looking at?"

"Good-morning, Robert," said Honore. "What is it that seems to interest you so much?"

Tete-de-Fer seemed ill at ease with a spade in his hand, and he made a most villainous-looking gardener. He answered, awkwardly enough:

"It's an old bit of black satin. Looks as if it might have been a mask once."

Honore took it and examined it curiously.

"It is a mask. I wonder how it came here?"

Grace became very pale.

"Perhaps," Honore went on, "they had a masked ball here during the life-time of the old marquis, and this is a relic."

"The old marquis wasn't that sort," answered Tete-de-Fer. "He was too close-fisted for anything like a masked ball."

"Well, it came here, somehow," said Honore, carelessly; and, to Grace's relief, he started to move on.

Tete-de-Fer, however, seemed anxious to talk, and said, quickly:

"It might have come through a masked marriage."

Grace caught Honore by the arm.

He pretended to mistake her meaning.

"Romantic little woman, you want to hear about a masked marriage, I suppose. I'm afraid they don't have such things these days, and that mask doesn't look over a year old."

He turned to Tete-de-Fer.

"Why do you think of a masked marriage?"

" Oh, such things have been here."

" Two centuries ago, maybe, but not since that mask was made."

Tete-de-Fer shrugged his shoulders obstinately.

" There was one in this very chateau not much over three years ago."

Honore laughed good naturedly.

Grace listened breathlessly.

" Your lordship may laugh, but it is so. The mayor has often told me of it, and he performed the ceremony."

" He was joking, my good fellow. Never believe such stories."

Again Tete-de-Fer shrugged his shoulders.

" He was not joking. Why, I saw with my own eyes."

" Nay, then," laughed Honore. " If you saw the marriage yourself, I'll say no more."

" I did not say that. But I did see the men who were murdered after it."

" Why, Grace, this is a real romance. But you are pale, my darling, this talk of murders frightens you. We'll have no more of it. Save your story, my good fellow, for another day when you can tell it to me."

" Oh, no, Honore, no. Let me hear it with you. I—I—will be glad to hear it."

" Then, at least, let us go sit in the arbor and listen to it. Come!"

" No, no, not there—not there, Honore."

Tete-de-Fer laughed.

" Perhaps her ladyship knows it was there the murdered men were found?"

Grace felt her strength giving way.

How knowingly the evil-looking man stared at her!

" Why should I know?" she asked, faintly.

Tete-de-Fer shrugged his shoulders.

" Do you mean, then," demanded Honore, " that such a marriage and such murders did really take place?"

" I saw the dead men, and the mayor told me of the wedding. It must have been a rare sight. The lady, he said, was a beauty. Why, only the other day, when he had just seen her ladyship, he said, very respectfully, please your lordship, he said the woman might have been her ladyship's sister, excepting for her face, which he didn't see."

Grace clung to her husband, and listened as if fascinated.

"They were all masked, he said, and the man and woman seemed very fond of each other. But it was all a sham, for the woman was all the time preparing to have the man murdered."

"What?" almost shrieked Grace.

"Yes; all the time she was kissing and hugging him, and telling him how she loved him, she knew her brother was getting ready to have him murdered."

"It's false—false!"

Grace started up indignantly; but instantly recollecting herself, was filled with a terrible fear lest her words had betrayed her.

"Oh, Honore!" she moaned.

"You must not hear any more," said he; "let us return to the house."

He led her to the chateau, trying to cheer her with reassuring talk, saying the story could not be true, for it would be impossible that such a marriage could take place.

"However, if you wish I will make inquiries."

"No; don't dear. I don't care to know. But, oh, Honore! it could not be true, could it, that any woman would do as that man said?"

"Of course not. She would have been a fiend. But, then, if she was married in a mask, she must have had a bad motive."

"Indeed, Honore, she had not."

"Why, my little Grace," he exclaimed, with a smile, "what an enthusiastic champion you are for this imaginary woman."

Poor Grace could hardly repress a cry as this second evidence of knowledge escaped her.

She was glad at that moment to have the footman, who had been to the town, hand Honore a letter.

"From the bank, Grace. May I read it?"

"Certainly."

CHAPTER XLIX.

NEWS OF ALPHONSE.

While Honore opened and read the letter, Grace recalled the words of Tete-de-Fer.

"Her brother was getting ready to have him murdered."

Was it possible, she asked herself in horror, that Alphonse could really have had Clinton Hastings killed?"

Then she remembered how a man had forced money from Alphonse in America.

This thought made her start:

Could this man, Robert, be the one?

He was a bad-looking man, and might be a murderer.

Did he know that she was the woman?

And, if he did, was he taking this way of letting her know it?

She grew faint at the thought of being in the power of that man.

"I will confess everything to Honore," she said to herself, "rather than permit that wicked creature to use his knowledge to make me purchase safety from him. Honore may spurn me from him, but, at least, I can always love him."

Looking at her husband's face, she saw that he was deeply agitated over the contents of the letter.

Presently he rose from his seat and went to a window, as if to look out.

Grace suspected that it was only to hide his agitation.

Full of fears about her secret, she at once became fearful that this letter might relate to that subject, for it seemed to her that from every quarter witnesses were rising up against her.

"What is the matter, Honore?"

He made no answer.

Grace hastened to his side.

"Something is wrong, Honore. Tell me what it is? Does it concern me?"

He nodded his head mournfully and gazed compassionately at her

Her imagination, in its feverish condition, made her anticipate the worst.

" Tell me?"

She could scarcely articulate the words, and her eyes were filled with pleading and terror.

" It is Alphonse," said Honore.

What an infinite relief the words were to her.

" What has he done?"

Honore put his arm around her.

" I hardly dare to tell you, my poor Grace. You must know some time, I suppose; but you seem so pale and nervous, I think I had better wait."

" Tell me now, Honore, the suspense will be worse than any shock."

" Read this letter, then."

The letter was as follows:

" The time has come when my duty to society compels me to take decisive steps in regard to your brother-in-law, Alphonse Gorinot. I hold forged checks of his to the amount of over fifty thousand francs. I can only postpone a notification to the proper authority until I hear from you. You have my heartfelt sympathy in this trouble, but I must warn you that no entreaties can now move me."

Alphonse a forger!" exclaimed Grace.

Honore nodded " Yes."

" And whose name has he forged, then?"

" Mine."

" Oh, Honore, how could he be so wicked! And have you suspected it before?"

" Alas! yes. It was a fear of this that made me wish to have him here with us."

" But what can have induced him to resort to such means. Surely he might have been content with the income you so generously gave him."

Honore seemed to hesitate.

" Perhaps it will be better if I tell you all I know," he said, finally.

" Please do!"

" It is very little, but it aids me to find a cause for his actions. It was by a mere accident that I learned of it.

" It seems that some time before we left Paris he became infatuated with a very beautiful but unprincipled woman, the wife, I believe, of a disreputable American artist.

"This artist, I think, used his knowledge of this infatuation to extort money from Alphonse.

"At any rate, he approached Alphonse one day when we were talking together on the street, and Alphonse, in some terror and annoyance, as it seemed to me, stepped aside with him and held a whispered conversation.

"What was said I don't know, except that the artist, whom I knew by sight, became angry and said, loud enough for me to hear, on purpose, I think:

"'You must. Remember the 13th of November, 1865.'

"'Hush!' exclaimed Alphonse. 'I will!'"

Grace, who had been growing more and more ghastly every moment, seemed now about to lose consciousness.

Seeing which, Honore led her to a seat, and said, tenderly:

"There, my darling; I knew this was not fit for you to hear. Let us say no more about it."

"I—I am—am better—now," she gasped, making a pitiful effort to recall her strength. "Please—go—on. I—I think I'd—better—hear it—all."

"Poor, dear little Grace! Don't take it too much to heart. It is sad for Alphonse, but we will live here retired from the world, and——"

"Yes, dear; yes," she interrupted, nervously patting his hand. "But—but this artist—did you learn his name!"

"I did, dear. Let me see. Was it Fulton? No, that wasn't it. Clinton? Yes, it was Clinton. No; it was Hastings. That's it—Clinton Hastings."

A moan fell from Grace's white lips.

"Poor fellow!" continued Honore. Just before we came away he was found dead in his bed—poisoned, the papers said."

"Alphonse did it!" shrieked Grace.

Honore rose to his feet with a look of horror on his face.

"Don't, Honore! Oh, don't! Stay with me! Please stay with me. If you leave me I shall go mad. I am innocent, indeed I am."

She fell on her knees and clasped her hands supplicatingly.

To her excited imagination, it seemed that her husband must suspect her.

"Grace, my darling," he said, as he lifted her up, "don't go on so. Your wretched brother's misdeeds need not affect you. Oh, I am angry when I think of all the shame that must fall on my pure and innocent wife because of that worthless fellow."

"But, Honore, I must tell you——"

"You must tell me nothing now, darling."

"Oh, Honore, if you only knew."

"There, my darling, there!"

It was as if he was talking to a little child.

"I must tell you now."

Grace felt that she must unburden her aching heart and satisfy her conscience.

Honore, however, refused to listen, and at last the worn-out, heart-weary woman acquiesced, and sat looking at her husband in dumb despair.

"Grace, dear," he said, after several minutes of reflection, "I think it will be better for me to hurry to Paris, and do what I can to aid your miserable brother. It may not be too late."

Grace offered no opposition.

The succession of shocks coming to her had plunged her into a sort of stupor.

Her senses were benumbed by excessive suffering.

Honore hastily prepared for his departure.

Grace embraced him mechanically, but he did not seem to notice it.

"I will walk to the station," he said.   "I have time enough, and the exercise will be good for me."

"Yes," she answered.

He embraced her for a last time, and was gone.

She mechanically waved an answering kiss to him as he passed through the gate.

But long after he had gone she stood on the marble steps, gazing vacantly into space.

She was still standing there when her maid came to announce the midday meal.

"Will your ladyship come into dinner?" she asked.

"Yes," she said, without moving, "I will come."

"It is waiting, your ladyship."

"We all have to wait; but the time will come."

The startled maid cast a quick glance at her mistress, and was shocked to see her pallor.

"You are ill, my lady," she said, gently, "may I assist you?"

She gave Grace her arm and carefully led her to the dining-room.

Grace ate the meal unconsciously almost, and then went to her room and locked herself in.

"Murder and deceit," she murmered. "Murder and deceit."

She searched in one of her closets.

The same blank expression filled her eyes, and she did not cease to repeat:

"Murder and deceit."

When she emerged from the closet she held one of her husband's pistols in her hand.

"Murder and deceit. Everything is red with blood. It is on my hands."

She cocked the pistol.

"When Honore returns he will know all about it. He would not let me tell him. Now Alphonse, the murderer, will tell him. Honore will be angry with his Grace. I could not bear that. I will die now, and when he comes he will be sorry. He will miss his little Grace, but he can never know how she loved him.

"Good-by, Honore darling."

CHAPTER L.

TETE-DE-FER HEARS FROM PARIS.

"Well, *ami*, have you told the marquis and the lady the story yet?'

"I have just told it."

"Good. You may go to Paris now, if you wish, though I would advise you not to."

"Why?"

Tete-de-Fer knew Bras-de-Fer's ways so well that he suspected something unpleasant.

Bras-de-Fer shrugged his shoulders.

"Elise has moved, I am told."

"Where to?"

"I do not know."

"Why did she move?"

"Oh, come now, *ami*, if you are going to be so fierce I will not dare to go on."

He laughed.

Tete-de-Fer feared all that jealousy could suggest.

"'Tell me," he shouted, "tell me why she moved."

"Ho, ho! Does Tete-de-Fer use that tone to me?"

"It is your doing, devil, that she has left me. It was for this you sent me from Paris."

Tete-de-Fer, with his blood on fire, flung down his gardener's tools and was rushing away.

"Stop, *ami.*"

Furious as he was, he could not overcome the spell of that imperious tone.

He stopped.

"Do you command me to tell you why she moved, or do you humbly beg me to tell you?"

"I beg it."

"Are you sorry for using that tone to me?"

"I am sorry."

"Ah! this is more like my gentle Tete-de-Fer!"

Tete-de-Fer was furiously gnawing his mustache.

"Well, listen, then, and I will tell you—only you must be calm. Will you be calm?"

"*Mon Dieu!* Do not torture me."

"But will you be calm?"

"Yes."

He looked like a raging wild beast.

"Do you remember that handsome young French American whom you got the money from in America?—the man of the secret, masked marriage?"

"Yes, yes."

"He was very handsome, was he not?"

Bras-de-Fer spoke meditatively.

Tete-de-Fer fairly danced.

"Will you tell me, wretch, about Elise?"

"'Tut, tut! my good Robert; you must not call names."

"Oh! *Grand Dieu!* But you are driving me crazy, and I do not know what I say."

"You are very sorry, then, for calling me a wretch?"

"I am, I am. But tell me—tell me!"

"Well, that handsome young man saw the pretty Elise. You would be delighted to see what a lovely couple they make on the Boulevard. People turn round and say——"

"Fiend! fiend! fiend!" howled Tete-de-Fer, striding furiously away.

"Stop, *ami!*"

Tete-de-Fer kept on.

"*Stop, Ami!*"

He stopped.

"Come back!"

He retraced his steps.

"You called me fiend—are you sorry?"

"Yes."

"You are so hasty, Robert. Now, listen. You cannot blame Elise. He gives her everything she asks—fine apartments—a whole suite, fitted up for a princess—horses, carriage, jewels, and such clothes!"

The thought of another being loved by Elise was maddening to Tete-de-Fer.

"I will kill her."

"You talk like a child. You can't kill her—you know it. If you could, it would do you no good. If I were you, I would make her stop loving him."

"How?"

"By making him ugly. He is now so handsome."

"How can I?"

"You never heard of Cæsar, of course. He was a wise general of olden times. He told his old soldiers to strike at the faces of the handsome young Romans in the army. They did, and they were successful."

"You want me to cut his face?"

"I want you to do nothing. I merely tell you a story. You may do as you please. By the way, a knife is an ugly thing, but it is useful sometimes. Have you one?"

"Yes."

"Let me see it."

Tete-de-Fer gave it to him.

"Pshaw! That is not sharp at all. If you like, you may have this nice one. It belonged to our handsome young friend once. Perhaps you remember it."

"It is the one he stuck into me."

"Yes. Now go."

"You have not told me where she lives."

"True."

"Will you tell me?"

"Inquire at her former apartment."

"You are not going back?"

"It seems to me that you are inquiring into my business."

"I may go, then?"

"Yes; but in your place I would take with me that crazy mayor's money. You may need it for pretty Elise."

CHAPTER LI.

ELISE AND ALPHONSE.

It was as Bras-de-Fer had said; Elise no longer lived in one modest apartment in a quiet quarter of the city.

She was sumptuously installed in a magnificent suite.

She wore only silks and satins, and her dazzling beauty was remarked on the Boulevard.

Alphonse was a devoted but not happy lover.

Elise had told him that she feared but one man, and he soon discovered it.

She had treated him with humiliating scorn, or easy carelessness, just as the mood took her.

She made him wait upon her like a lackey, and when he asked for some reward, told him he ought to be satisfied with the pleasure of serving her.

If he complained too loudly, she threatened to close her doors against him.

The day succeeding the enlightenment of Tete-de-Fer, Alphonse was earnestly beseeching her not to torment him any longer.

"You said you would love me if I killed the artist."

"Bah! what an ugly word. But you are mistaken; I only said I would try."

"You have not even tried."

"I have not dared."

"Why?"

"You have asked for my love, but you have not asked me to be your wife."

"Wife!"

"Yes, wife. Wicked wretch, do you dare to tell me——"

"Ah! Elise, you are only making an excuse for getting angry with me."

"An excuse! Not your wife! Will you leave my house? Not his wife! Oh! Heaven! how he insults me."

Elise was in a magnificent passion.

"I did not mean it, Elise. I will marry you if you wish it."

"He will marry me if I wish it! *Mon Dieu!* As if I were begging him to marry me. There is the door."

She pointed to it in indignation.

"Will you hear me, Elise?"

Alphonse was very humble.

"Go on, but do not venture to insult me again."

"I should be only too glad to make you my wife. You know I adore you and live for you alone."

"Mere talk."

"Have I not proved it?"

He looked around the richly furnished apartments.

"Did you think, then, that you had purchased me like a slave?"

"You know I did not mean that. I would give you ten times as much if I had it, and think myself happy if you would take it."

"Bah!"

"Will you be my wife, my beautiful Elise?"

A servant entered the room.

"A gentleman would like to see mademoiselle."

"Where is he?"

"In the reception-room."

"What name?"

"He would not give it, but said it was about urgent business that he wished to see you."

"Tell him I know of no business. I am engaged."

"Pardon me, but I must see you."

It was the Marquis d'Iberri who stepped mournfully into the room.

"Honore!" exclaimed Alphonse, overcome by his guilty fears.

"How dare you?"

Elise did not recognize Bras-de-Fer.

"Forgive me, mademoiselle," said Honore, sadly, "if I force myself upon you. This man," pointing to Alphonse, "will tell you that I have a right to be here, since it was my money paid for all this."

"Who are you, then?"

Alphonse did not speak. He hung his head in fear and shame.

"I am the Marquis d'Iberri."

"Well, and what of that?"

"Alphonse, tell this lady that I must see you alone for a few minutes."

Alphonse hesitated; he dreaded an outbreak from the human tigress.

"Well," she said, scornfully surveying him, "why do you not tell this gentleman that he has made a mistake, and that this is my house, in which, without my permission, nobody holds secret conferences."

"Alphonse, please go into that room. I wish to say a few words in explanation to this lady."

Glad to escape even for a moment, Alphonse hastily retired before Elise could stop him.

"Well, monsieur," she exclaimed, turning to the marquis, "explain, then, why you come into my house and give orders."

"It is I, Elise—Bras-de-Fer. Hush!"

"I am glad to see you. How handsome and grand you are! Oh, let me have a good look at you. Always a man."

Elise greedily studied his face and poured out her words of love and admiration like the savage creature she was.

She seemed to care nothing that he did not love her.

"I must see him at once. Robert is on his way here. After him the officers are coming."

"Robert is coming? Pshaw! but we shall have a circus, and my poor little man in there?"

Robert knows what he is to do about him."

"And the officers?"

"They will take Robert only. I will save the other one."

"And I?"

"When I snap my fingers so, you will come to me and say you love me."

"And you will put your arm around me?"

"Strange woman! Yes."

"Good. I will do it."

"Have you a room for me as I told you, with all my traps in it?"

"Exactly as you told me."

"You have been a good girl, Elise."

He held out his hand.

She seized it and covered it with kisses.

'I am repaid," she said.

CHAPTER LII.

TETE-DE-FER ALMOST FORGETS CÆSAR.

"Alphonse, I know all about the forgeries."

"Forgive me, D'Iberri, I——"

"Forgive you? Unfortunately this is the easiest part of it. The bank has notified me that the police have the matter in hand. Any moment they may track you here."

"*Mon Dieu!* What shall I do?

"Have you any money?"

"No."

"Here are some bills. Now wait till I am gone. Then slip out of the house, and get to D'Iberri if you can. You will be safe there."

"Oh, how can I thank you?"

"Think of that later."

Honore passed quickly into the next room where Elise awaited him.

"Keep him here till Robert comes. Stop! I have forgotten something."

He ran back to Alphonse, and taking from under his coat a stout club, handed it to him.

"You may be in need of something like this. Do not be captured."

Alphonse glanced hastily at the club and wished it was a knife.

He waited long enough to let Honore get out of the house.

In the next room he found Elise pacing up and down in a most furious state.

She would not listen to what he said, but poured out upon him a flood of angry exclamations.

He tried to get away, but like a tigress she sprang before him and barred his way.

He pleaded; she stormed.

Finally her quick ear caught the sound of an altercation near the door.

At once she threw herself into Alphonse's arms, and began to lavish caresses on him.

Tete-de-Fer bounded into the room with a yell of rage more like what might come from a wild beast.

Elise cast Alphonse away from her, and with one hand hidden in the folds of her dress, leaned against the center-table, with a smile of curiosity on her face.

The two men looked at each other.

Alphonse stared in wild fear at Tete-de-Fer. He had thought him dead.

Tete-de-Fer turned to Elise.

"You love him—him, a little toy-man?"

Elise laughed merrily. She enjoyed the rage of this brute.

"At least, he is good-looking."

"Then I will spoil his looks."

Tete-de-Fer made a frightful effort to adopt the careless, mocking tone of his Bras-de-Fer.

"Look you, my pretty face," he said to Alphonse, "do you see this little knife? You left it sticking in my ribs once. I am going to carve you now."

His eyes glared ferociously.

Alphonse knew he could not escape.

He drew the club from under his coat and took a wary attitude.

This only enraged Tete-de-Fer.

He sprang at Alphonse to clutch him by the throat.

Alphonse struck fiercely at him and hit him on the head.

Tete-de-Fer staggered.

A little stream of blood trickled over his forehead.

Alphonse anticipated victory. He tried to smile at Elise.

Tete-de-Fer intercepted the smile and was crazy.

Reckless of the club, he sprang once more at Alphonse, and in spite of the struggles of the latter caught him by the throat.

He forgot the story of Cæsar for a moment, and buried the dagger in the body of Alphonse.

Alphonse staggered; his legs gave way under him, and he sank.

Tete-de-Fer then remembered Cæsar, and deliberately slit the nose of the unfortunate wretch.

Even Elise turned sick at that, and cried out·
"You brute!"
"Ah! It shall be your turn now."
He was drunk with blood and excitement.
He arose from the bleeding body and rushed at Elise.
She merely stiffened her arm, and held the shining point
of her dagger straight before her.
Tete-de-Fer stopped short. He knew a scratch would
suffice to kill him.
"*Ami.*"
Bras-de-Fer stood in the door-way.
"The police are coming up stairs. If you love freedom
go out the back way."
Tete-de-Fer hesitated. He was unable to think clearly.
"Oh, well, if you prefer to stay, all right."
"No, no. Which way shall I go?"
"Out that door."
Tete-de-Fer disappeared.
"Quick, now, Elise. To your old apartment. Get my
bed ready for him."
Elise left without a word.
Bras-de-Fer took Alphonse in his arms, and quietly car-
ried him down stairs and put him into a carriage.
The police were after Tete-de-Fer, and had captured
him.
The bank cashier had not yet made a complaint against
Alphonse.
In forgetting Cæsar, Tete-de-Fer had spoiled Clinton's
plans.

CHAPTER LIII.

WHAT HAPPENED AT D'IBERRI.

Grace lifted the pistol. Her finger was on the trigger.
Her eyes fell upon a picture of her husband.
She uttered a cry.
Since her husband had kissed her good-by, her eyes had
been fixed on vacancy. She had lived a dream—a dream of
guilt.
The pistol fell from her hand. She burst into tears.
She was scarcely conscious of the crime she had almost
committed, but she shuddered when she looked at the pis-
tol.

"I was out of my mind," she whispered. "Thank Heaven I did not do it! When Honore returns I will tell him everything. This time I will. He shall not prevent me. Better anything than this daily torture. Why, I am almost crazy."

She grew calmer. It was a desperate sort of calmness—such a calmness as a condemned man might summon up to meet death with.

She tested her strength and went into the dreaded rooms.

If Honore would forgive her, she would learn to love these rooms for his sake.

"But no," she said to herself; "I must not think of that. He will not forgive me. Well, then, I shall die. I could not live without his love."

The time dragged slowly along until the next day at noon, when a letter from Honore was brought to her.

He said little about Alphonse, but filled his letter with words of love and longing for his little wife. He would be home that night.

Grace kissed the dear letter as if it were all that remained to her of her love. Indeed, she almost had that feeling.

The hours now seemed to drag more slowly than ever, and yet they sped by with frightful rapidity.

She wished to see her husband and she dreaded to.

She wandered aimlessly about the chateau, and at length made her way to the square chamber, where she sat down, and, in memory, went over the events of that night so few years ago.

A footstep at that moment caused her to look up.

Clinton Hastings stood before her.

She stared at him for a moment wildly; then recovered her composure, like one who had suffered all and was now callous.

"Are you not dead, then?" she asked.

"No, base woman! I am alive, and I come here to remind you of your words of the 13th of November three years ago. By this ring"—he held up a sapphire ring—"I claim you for my wife!"

He waited, but she did not open her lips. Her heart was numb with the exquisite pain she suffered.

This, however, must be the last. Her husband had come to claim her, and now all was over with her.

"You do not answer. Do you dispute my claim to you?"

"No."

She spoke without excitement.

"And you will go with me?"

"I will."

"Come, then."

"I must beg you to grant me a few hours in which to prepare. I would like to write a letter to my—to the Marquis d'Iberri. I would like to explain to him why I go."

"Where will you meet me, and when?"

"It is for you to name the time and place. I will be punctual."

"No. 27 Rue d'Artois, Paris; third floor; at 9 o'clock to-morrow morning."

"I will be there."

"Without fail?"

"Without fail."

Clinton left the room. Where he went or how he had found his way there mattered not to Grace.

It was enough for her that he had come.

She accepted her fate. She had been at fault. Maybe Heaven would be satisfied now. She had suffered all she could, and might be allowed to die, perhaps.

Everything Honore had given her she put aside, first tenderly kissing each object.

She shed no tears.

She made no effort to collect any clothing to take with her. She put on a plain traveling-dress.

Then she sat down and wrote a letter to Honore. She would not allow herself to think of what he would say, or do, or think.

She was not his wife, and never could be now.

Innocent as she was of intentional wrong, she was so affected by all the harrowing events of the past few days that she had come to look upon herself as a guilty woman.

She sealed the letter, kissed it, and placed it on a little table where Honore could not fail to see it.

Then she put on her bonnet and calmly left the room.

The moment she was gone, Clinton slipped through the secret door in the wall, took the letter, and disappeared.

Grace ordered the carriage, and leaving word that she would not return for some time, was driven to the station.

On the same train that took Grace to Paris was Bras-de-Fer.

He watched her closely all the way to the hotel in Paris, where, having seen her registered as Mrs. Hastings, he left her, feeling that she was not intending to play him false.

How to account for her calmness he did not know. In his diseased frame of mind he sought only for an unworthy reason.

He was so filled with the idea that Grace was playing a part, that every loving impulse that sprang from his heart and prompted him to forego his revengeful designs, he angrily put aside as a weakness.

Now that his carefully prepared vengeance was about to be consummated he was unable to retain any sort of internal composure.

His brain was in a whirl. He strode along the streets without taking heed of where he was going.

He had not yet read the letter which Grace had written. He could guess what it would be, and had no curiosity to read it.

All night he walked, keeping up all the time a fight against his better self, which told him that he should pause.

Every suggestion to good he treated as a temptation from the evil one.

Day was dawning when he re-entered Paris and made his way to Rue d'Artois.

CHAPTER LIV.

AN OLD STORY RETOLD.

Clinton knocked at the door of Elise's apartment.
She let him in.
" How is Alphonse?"
" Much better. The wound is not fatal."
" Then he can hear what I have to tell him?"
" Yes."
" I will go in then."
" Bras-de-Fer."
" Yes, Elise."
" You did not snap your fingers the other day."

He smiled sadly. He could not even pretend to make any return for the blind worship of this wild creature.

"No, Elise, I did not expect Robert to strike so hard. Perhaps I may snap my fingers to-day."

He went into the next room. Alphonse looked at him in surprise.

"You here!" he exclaimed, feebly.

Clinton shrugged his shoulders. He forgot that he was Bras-de-Fer.

"Where should I be?"

Alphonse was still more surprised.

Neither manner nor voice was Bras-de-Fer's.

Clinton became conscious that he was not acting his part properly. But what did it matter now.

"You think I am Bras-de-Fer. Undeceive yourself, I am Clinton Hastings."

Alphonse started.

"Yes, I am your brother-in-law, and I am going to tell you a story."

The door leading into the other room was suddenly thrown open and Elise sprang in.

"Robert is here."

"Escaped?"

"Yes."

"Good. Heaven is kind, or otherwise, to send him here to hear my story. By and by she will be here too. Let him come in. Ah! There he is. Welcome, *ami*. We are well met. I was just going to tell this sick man a story. You may listen.

Tete-de-Fer stared about him in stupefied amazement.

Elise sat down and enjoyed the scene. It was a perfect delight to her to watch the masterful ways of Bras-de-Fer. Then, too, she hoped now that he would snap his fingers.

"What does it mean?"

Tete-de-Fer pointed to Alphonse, and glanced about the room comprehensively as if his question included everything.

"It means this."

Clinton with his marvelous dexterity and strength had suddenly caught Tete-de-Fer and pinned his arms behind him.

Tete-de-Fer uttered an imprecation and made an effort to free himself.

"Quiet, *ami*, or I'll twist your arms.   Elise bring me a rope.   I must tie this wild beast or he may not be willing to stay here and listen to my story."

Elise brought a rope from her room.

With his arms bound Tete-de-Fer leaned sullenly against the wall.

Alphonse had viewed the strange occurrence with increasing fear.

He began to see how completely he had been duped and played with.

Clinton placed himself so that he could see the two men, and they could see him.

"I am going to tell you a story, you two.   Part of it you know, part of it you do not.

"On the 13th of November, 1865, a poor artist was trapped into a marriage.   I need not describe the ceremony.

"He was taken from his wife blindfolded.   That had been agreed upon.

"Three men set upon him to kill him.   He killed two of them and escaped.

"He swore he would be avenged.   He needed money to do anything; but he was patient.   He took the money which had been paid to the hired assassins, and went to California and speculated.   In two years he was worth millions.

"He was very lucky in that and other things, as you will see.

"He hunted for the people who had injured him, and found them, excepting, of course, the two who were dead.

"Who are they?   Listen.

"Grace Howard, Alphonse Gorinot, Robert Caradoc, and the Mayor of D'Iberri.

The mayor, luckily for him, is crazy.   I used one of the offenders to punish him.

"Robert Caradoc, now that you know me, you can say if I have made you suffer.

"I have used you to punish the others, and have not ceased to torment you.   I found out what was dearest to you and struck you there.

"It was through me that Elise met him and cast you aside.

"Alphonse Gorinot, you are more guilty. See how I have made you pay for your villainy."

He quickly stripped from his face the peculiarities of Bras-de-Fer, and showed Alphonse the features of the Marquis d'Iberri.

Alphonse gasped and stared, but spoke no word.

"I have made your life a torment. Every evil thing that has happened to you has come through me. I need not rehearse what has happened.

"But even that wound and disfigurement you owe to me. I gave him the knife—your own knife—to do it with; just as I gave you the club he tried to murder me with, and with which you tried to break his head.

"If you live it will be in prison. He, too, will spend his life in prison.

"And now see; the woman you two have been committing your violence for, loves neither of you, she loves me.

"Is it not so, Elise?"

He snapped his fingers, and she sprang lovingly into his arms.

At this Tete-de-Fer made a frightful effort to burst his bonds.

He could not break them, but he did loosen them, and he took advantage of the fact.

He quietly and persistently worked away until his arms were free. No one had observed what he was doing. He bided his time.

In the meantime Clinton had put the reluctant Elise away from him and turned to Alphonse.

"It will not hurt your selfish soul to know about Grace, but in order that you may learn how complete my vengeance has been, I will tell you that she, the most guilty, has already suffered more than any of you.

"I have gone to her at last as Clinton Hastings, and forced her to leave the luxury of D'Iberri. She does not know, and shall never know, that her two husbands are the same person. She shall live in misery with me, believing that the Marquis d'Iberri, whom she loves, I believe, loathes and scorns her."

He had forgotten Tete-de-Fer, and had his back to him.

A scream from Elise made him turn, just in time to see Tete-de-Fer plunge a knife into her breast.

One leap took Clinton to the side of the monster.

With one hand he snatched the knife from the wound, and with the other caught Tete-de-Fer by the throat.

Elise fell dying on the floor.

Tete-de-Fer fell by her side, pierced to the heart.

Clinton tenderly lifted the dying woman's head.

She smiled up at him.

"I loved you, didn't I?" she murmured.

Tears rolled down the stern face of the hard man, as he nodded yes.

"Will you kiss me now. I am dying, you know?"

He leaned over her and pressed a kiss upon her lips.

She smiled.

She was dead.

CHAPTER LV.

A PART OF THE SAME STORY.

"Is she dead?"

It was a whisper from Alphonse.

"Yes."

"He, too?"

"Yes."

"I am dying."

Clinton looked coldly at him.

"It is the best thing you can do."

"I suppose it is, but I must tell you what you do not know."

"If you wish. I do not care to hear it."

"You will forever regret it if you do not. I want to tell you why Grace married you. My mother married Alphonse Gorinot, my father, against the wishes, but with the reluctant consent of her father. My father abused my mother by neglecting her. Her father would have nothing to do with them after their marriage. My father died. My mother then took me and went to live with her father. He did not like me, and said I was my father's child. At her father's entreaty my mother married an American gentleman, Grace's father. The marriage was a very happy one, and my grandfather was delighted. When Grace was born he devoted himself to her. When he died he left his money, a goodly fortune to her. Our mother had enough already. A provision of the will was that Grace could have

the money only in case she married an American. Our
father and mother died, and Grace and I were brought up
in America by Mr. Howard's sister. As I grew older I
wished for money, but Miss Howard would give me none,
and though I got all Grace had, it was not enough. I
learned of the will one day, and set about studying how I
could get some of the money. I knew that if Grace had
the money I, too, could have plenty, for she was very generous, and very fond of me. I knew also that any husband
she might have would probably take care that I did not
squander her money. Then I thought of the plan of
having some starving American in France—there are always
plenty, you know—marry her for a sum of money, without
knowing who she was, and then leaving her. I had great
difficulty in persuading Grace to accede to my plan, but
finally, by putting it in its most romantic light and treating
it as a frolic, I succeeded. For a whole year I plotted and
planned without avail until by accident I learned of you.
I studied your ways and knew you thoroughly, as you will
remember. I was sure you would consent. Then Grace
and I and Miss Howard lived quietly and unknown in the
parish, and I had the banns published. Miss Howard, however, did not suspect a thing. I got Daddy Braune to find
me this man and two other as witnesses. And when I
found out what sort of a fellow he was, I used him to nego-
tiate with the mayor. To make Grace better satisfied, I
hired the D'Iberri chateau. She never knew its name, nor
where it was, for I knew the mystery of secrecy would please
her. That is why she never was startled by your title. I
see now you bought it. I never suspected you, though I
felt that it was a strange chance that made you marry
Grace. A strange freak took Grace that night, and she fell
in love with you, as you will remember, though you may
have doubted it since. She acted with such infatuation,
that I suspected she had broken her promise and I arranged
with this man to kill you. Grace knew not a word of it.
He assured me you were dead, and after a while I told
Grace of it. She mourned for a while, and then—she was
very young—she forgot, I suppose. You know all the
rest."

The agony suffered by Clinton Hastings during that re-
cital cannot be measured in words.

One by one the tortures he had inflicted on his gentle

wife came up before him, and one by one they racked his soul.

He took no heed of the dying man.   He paced the chamber, stepping at each turn with hideous unconsciousness over the two dead bodies.

"Great Heaven!" he exclaimed, "can I ever atone for this awful sin against one of your angels.   Grace, Grace, my darling wife, can you look at me again without loathing?"

He suddenly thought of her letter in his pocket. He hurriedly drew it out and tore it open.

"My Darling Honore :—You may cease to love me when you read this letter.   I expect that, for I no longer have any right to your love; but you may be able to forgive me.   Please do so if you can."

After that followed a succinct story of her marriage to Clinton Hastings.

She plainly said that at that moment a sudden and real love for her husband had sprung up in her heart.   She could not explain it, but she would confess it.

She made no attempt to excuse herself or shift blame or responsibility on Alphonse.   Then she went on:

"When I first saw you, my Honore—please let me call you so until this letter is finished.   When I close this letter my love and my life will both go out.

"When I first saw you, my darling, I loved you, and I have loved you with an increasing love ever since.

"I knew you loved me, and I hoped and dreaded to have you tell me of it.

"I thought I was free to marry you, but I also knew I had no right to do so with a secret like mine locked in my heart.

"That dreadful but ever blessed night, when in the midst of death you spoke the love I felt, I was supremely happy.

"I thought we were going to death together, and that I need not risk your contempt by telling my secret.

"After we were saved I tried to gain courage several times to tell you, but you spoke so vehemently about any previous love that I lost my heart and weakly held my tongue.

"Oh, Honore, if you could but realize how I have suffered since, you would forgive me.

"My heart is bruised and sore, and now the blows that fall upon it are no longer felt.

"My husband, Clinton Hastings, has come for me, and I must go to him.

"But I cannot live long now.   I know it, and it is my only happiness.

"Honore, my dear, dear Honore,
          "Once your wife, your   GRACE."

"Oh, Heaven!" groaned Clinton. "Blind fool, sodden in my own self-sufficiency, I sought to usurp your prerogative, and I am fitly punished."

He fell upon his knees.

"Oh, Heaven!" he prayed, "let me atone for this to the patient creature who has borne all my fiendish torture without even murmur of complaint. My life shall be devoted to her happiness if you will but permit me to still have her love. I do not deserve it, but, oh, Heaven! give it to me."

He rose to his feet.

"Gracious Heaven! she may be here at any moment, Alphonse."

Alphonse had gone with Tete-de-Fer and Elise to make a final accounting of his misdeeds.

With feverish haste Clinton threw off the clothes that made him look like any other than Honore, and listening to every footfall with terrified anxiety, he at last was ready.

Locking the door on the scene of death he hastened down stairs.

Grace had just begun to question the porter.

At that moment she saw Honore.

CHAPTER LVI.

WHAT HAPPENED THEN.

"Honore!" gasped Grace."

"Yes, darling, I. Let us go away from here."

"Have you been to D'Iberri?"

"Yes, darling, and received your letter. Poor suffering little Grace. I know everything. More even than you do. Come."

Grace shook her head sadly.

"I cannot go with you, Honore. I promised my—Clinton Hastings that I would come to him."

"I know it, my darling. I have seen him, and he will meet us at D'Iberri."

"Honore, you have never yet deceived me. You will not do it now?"

Clinton groaned when he thought how he had done nothing else but deceive the pure and trusting woman.

"Grace, I swear to you that I speak the truth."

"You need not swear, Honore, your word is enough."

There was an infinite sadness in her sweet voice.

He led her to a cab, and they were driven to a railway.

When they reached D'Iberri, Clinton insisted that Grace should eat something.

Then he led the way to the square chamber. Grace did not even shudder now.

Not once had he made any demonstration of affection. She would not have permitted it.

"Grace," he said, "I have brought you here purposely to tell you something before Clinton Hastings comes. You have been terribly tortured by that man."

"Don't, Honore. I deserve it all for my weakness. I will not say guilt, for I intended no wrong."

"Everything you have suffered has been of his doing. He has pursued you like a fiend.

"He is sorry for it now, for he knows you are as pure and innocent as an angel.

"He thought then that you were in league with Alphonse to murder him that night.

"He escaped death providentially, and he swore vengeance in this very room.

"I want to plead for him, Grace. I want to know if you can forgive him for what he has done."

"He was justified, Honore. If there is anything for me to forgive I do it freely."

"All the while he was making you suffer he loved you, Grace. He loved you that night, and he has been well-nigh crazy since with the mad struggle between his love and his demoniac desire for revenge.

"Can you forgive him?"

"Everything, Honore."

"Can you love him?"

Grace raised her blue eyes and looked at Honore.

"No, I cannot love him."

"Why?"

"Can you ask me why, Honore? For the last time, it may be, let me say it. I love you, Honore, and only you; my heart is dead to everything else.

"Is it because he has been so cruel to you that you cannot love him."

"No. If I loved him his cruelty would not change me."

"Do you mean then that if you had loved him as you

love me, you would forgive his cruelty and love him still.

"Do you not know, Honore, that a woman loves? And that is the whole story. Cruelty is nothing. A woman merely loves."

"I will return in a moment, Grace.

He left the room.

In a short time Clinton Hastings stood before Grace. She looked at him inquiringly."

"WHATEVER THERE IS TO FORGIVE, AND I LOVE YOU AS WELL AS I DID YESTERDAY, AND THAT IS WITH MY WHOLE HEART, SOUL, AND BEING."

He passed his hand over his face and drew off the brown beard and wig.

"Grace, I am Clinton Hastings."

"You! you!"

She shut her eyes and spread her hands before her.

"Don't turn from me, darling. I have been wicked, and deserve only your hate.

"But, indeed, I truly love you, and always have, impossible as it may seem.

"Will you not look at me, Grace? Will you not forgive me? If any torture could compensate, I would readily undergo it to pay the penalty of my wickedness.

"I dare not ask for your love, Grace, but humbly I ask for a chance to make the remainder of your life happy.

"You cannot trust me, can you?"

He stood before her with bowed head.

"Honore—I will call you so—I cannot explain all this to myself. I feel as if I must doubt your word, when you tell me you made your loving Grace suffer as she has.

"But let it be so. It has proved my love. You can never doubt that now. Let all the past be dead, and we will begin a new life from this time."

"You forgive me then?"

"Whatever there is to forgive, and I love you as well as I did yesterday, and that is with my whole heart, soul, and being."

"Oh, my angel, Grace!"

[THE END.]

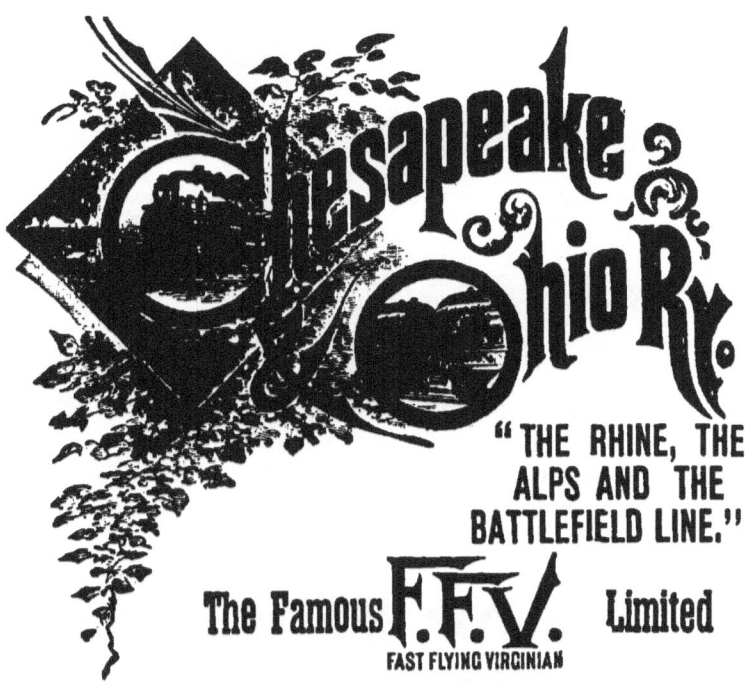

"THE RHINE, THE ALPS AND THE BATTLEFIELD LINE."

The Famous F.F.V. Limited
FAST FLYING VIRGINIAN

Has No Equal Between
CINCINNATI AND NEW YORK,
Via Washington, Baltimore, and Philadelphia.
Vestibuled, Steam Heated, and Electric Lighted Throughout.
THROUGH DINING CAR AND COMPLETE PULLMAN SERVICE.
THROUGH SLEEPERS TO AND FROM
ST. LOUIS, CHICAGO AND LOUISVILLE.

The most interesting historic associations and the most striking and beautiful scenery in the United States are linked together by the C. & O. System, which traverses Virginia, the first foothold of English settlers in America, where the Revolutionary War was begun and ended, and where the great battles of the Civil War were fought; crosses the Blue Ridge and Alleghany Mountains and the famous Shenandoah Valley, reaches the celebrated Springs region of the Virginias, and lies through the canons of New River, where the scenery is grand beyond description. It follows the banks of the Kanawha and Ohio Rivers, and penetrates the famous Blue Grass region of Kentucky, noted for producing the greatest race-horses of the world.

For maps, folders, descriptive pamphlets, etc., apply to Pennsylvania Railroad ticket offices in New York, Philadelphia, and Baltimore, the principal ticket offices throughout the country, or any of the following C. & O. agencies:

NEW YORK—362 and 1323 Broadway;
WASHINGTON—513 and 1421 Penna. avenue;
CINCINNATI—Corner Fifth and Walnut streets;
LOUISVILLE—253 Fourth avenue;
ST. LOUIS—Corner Broadway and Chestnut street;
CHICAGO—234 Clark street.

C. B. RYAN, Assistant General Passenger Agent, Cincinnati, O.
H. W. FULLER, General Passenger Agent, Washington. D. C.

New York and New England
RAILROAD.

Travelers between New York and Boston should always ask for tickets via the

"NEW ENGLAND LIMITED" TRAIN,

Leaving either city 3.00 P. M. DAILY, including SUNDAY, due destination 9.00 P. M.

Buffet Smoker, Parlor Cars and Coaches. Dining Car between Boston and Willimantic.

See that your tickets read via NEW YORK and NEW ENGLAND and "AIR LINE" ROUTE.

The Norwich Line,
INSIDE ROUTE.

Steamers leave Pier 40, North River, New York, 5.30 P. M. week days only. Connecting at New London with Vestibuled Steamboat Express Train due Worcester 8.00 A. M., Boston 9.00 A. M.

RETURNING,

Train leaves Boston 7.05 P. M. week days only. Connecting at New London with Steamers of the Line due New York 7.00 A. M.

Tickets, Parlor Car Seats, Staterooms on Steamers, and full information at offices,

353 Broadway,
Grand Central Station, } NEW YORK.
Pier 40, North River,

322 Washington St., } BOSTON.
Station foot of Summer St.,

GEO. F. RANDOLPH, General Traffic Manager, Boston.

W. B. BABCOCK, General Passenger Agent.

Jan. 11, 1894.

READING RAILROAD SYSTEM.

THE ROYAL BLUE LINE

between New York, Philadelphia, Baltimore, Wash·
ington, the South, and South-west is conceded to be
the BEST CONSTRUCTED and MOST FINELY
EQUIPPED RAILROAD in the country.

THE OLD RELIABLE ROUTE

to all points in Interior Pennsylvania—Reading,
Harrisburg, Gettysburg, Pottsville, Shamokin, and
Williamsport.

THE ROYAL ROUTE TO THE SEA.

The Double Track Line between Philadelphia and Atlantic City.

I. A. SWEIGARD, General Superintendent.

C. G. HANCOCK, General Passenger Agent.

TAKE

FOR ALL PRINCIPAL POINTS IN

MISSOURI,

KANSAS,

INDIAN TERRITORY,

TEXAS,

MEXICO, AND

CALIFORNIA.

FREE RECLINING CHAIR CARS ON ALL TRAINS.

Through Wagner Palace Buffet Sleeping Cars
from the **GREAT LAKES** to the
GULF OF MEXICO,

For further information call on or address your nearest
Ticket Agent, or

JAMES BARKER, G. P. & T. A.,

St. Louis, Mo.

www.ingramcontent.com/pod-product-compliance
Lightning Source LLC
Chambersburg PA
CBHW030538040726
47497CB00008B/2500